Teaching Listening and Speaking

A Handbook for English Language Teachers and Teacher Trainers

Kamlesh Sadanand

Orient BlackSwan

Acknowledgements

We are grateful to CNN-IBN for permission to use audio clips of some of their recordings. Every attempt has been made to trace copyright holders for other material used in this book but no information has been received at the time of going to press. The publishers would be grateful for information regarding copyright holders so that due acknowledgement can be made in all future editions of the book.

ORIENT BLACKSWAN PRIVATE LIMITED

Registered Office
3-6-752 Himayatnagar, Hyderabad 500 029 (A.P.), India
E-mail: centraloffice@orientblackswan.com

Other Offices
Bangalore, Bhopal, Bhubaneshwar, Chennai,
Ernakulam, Guwahati, Hyderabad, Jaipur, Kolkata,
Lucknow, Mumbai, New Delhi, Noida, Patna

First published 2012

ISBN 978 81 250 4659 2

Cover and book design

Typeset in Charter BT 11/13
OSDATA, Hyderabad 500 029

Printed in India at
Graphica Printers and Binders
Hyderabad 500 013

Published by
Orient Blackswan Private Limited
3-6-752 Himayatnagar, Hyderabad 500 029 (A.P.), India
E-mail: hyderabad@orientblackswan.com

Contents

Part II: Appendices

Preface

Until the last quarter of the twentieth century, teachers of English and educators perceived the learning of reading and writing as the most important need of their students. That explains the focus on reading, writing and the related subskills in English textbooks for schools. With the advent of globalisation, however, English language teaching has acquired a global perspective, and English is now widely accepted as an international language. There is, thus, an increasing demand for proficient speakers of the language in almost every field. Given the fact that proficiency in oral communication in English is essential for employment in India and abroad, the teaching of listening and speaking is now considered to be of great importance. These skills are included, though not significantly, as components of English courses and textbooks. The majority of the teachers who are required to teach the skills, however, have little or no guidance on how to do it. This handbook is a step in that direction.

The book, which has a part each on teaching listening and speaking, attempts to help teachers reflect on the nature of the two skills. The first part on teaching listening begins by drawing a distinction between listening and hearing on the one hand and different kinds of listening on the other. This is done by using dialogues in social contexts as illustrative examples, followed up with activities intended to create awareness of the functions of listening, or the purposes for which we listen in our daily lives. In the units that follow, recordings of television programmes are used as listening texts, and activities are designed to help teachers differentiate between the teaching of listening and its testing, so that they recognise that the former includes the process essential to meaningful listening. The activities are broad-based, giving attention to vocabulary and grammar and providing a link to speaking, which naturally follows listening.

The part on the teaching of speaking deals with the contexts in which we use spoken language. It underlines, through a series of dialogues, the importance of using appropriate language in addition to producing grammatical sentences in social and academic contexts for successful communication. In these dialogues, teachers are required to identify the inappropriate use of language in terms of the formal–informal cline, the attitudes of speakers and the types of sentences, and suggest changes to make them acceptable and appropriate. In the second unit, prompting is suggested as a useful technique to motivate the learner to speak. Visual and audio prompting is used to help teachers reflect on the usefulness of these techniques. The third unit concentrates on the use of functions in social and academic contexts. The activities are designed to enable teachers to relate the use of appropriate language to the functions performed.

I have attempted to provide in the book as much help as possible to teachers in the form of extensive notes, a section on pronunciation for easy reference, sample materials from textbooks with guidance on how to use them to teach listening and speaking to different levels of learners, an answer key to every unit and, on the accompanying CD, recordings of all the listening texts in the book, including those of television programmes.

Kamlesh Sadanand
April 2012

Part I

Listening

Unit 1

Hearing and Listening

When we consider 'listening' as an effective base in the language learning process, we in fact include 'hearing'. In other words, if we cannot hear something or somebody, it will not be possible for us to listen. Hearing is, therefore, assumed when we teach listening. Owing to this assumption, the distinction between the two tends to get blurred. However, for the purposes of language teaching, we need to understand the difference in their meanings.

Let us look at some contexts to understand the difference in meaning between 'listen' and 'hear'. First we shall construct contexts in which we hear.

Dialogue 1

A: You look like you haven't slept all night.

B: You're right. I didn't get a wink of sleep last night. It was the deafening rap music next door. Didn't you hear it?

A: Yes, I did. But nothing can keep me awake after eleven. I slept right through all that noise.

B: Lucky you!

Dialogue 2

A: Last evening Radha was terrified at the thought that someone was following her.

B: Was she? What happened?

A: She says she could hear footsteps behind her all the way home.

B: Did she find out who it was?

A: No. each time she turned round, there was no one in sight.

Notice that in these two contexts the speakers talk about 'hearing' as something that is more or less involuntary. Physiologically, our ears are structured to enable us to catch sounds, noise, etc., within earshot, whether we want to or not.

DIALOGUE 3

A: I'm going to a concert. Would you like to come?

B: Thank you so much. But I've heard these artists perform on the radio.

A: Did they? It must've been absorbing.

B: Yes, indeed.

DIALOGUE 4

A: Where are you off to?

B: I'm going to a panel discussion.

A: On what?

B: On the relevance of non-violence in the modern world.

A: But you've heard such discussions ever so often.

B: Even so. I'd like to hear what these panelists have to say.

In dialogues 3 and 4 the word 'hear' is used to mean 'listen to' or 'pay attention to' and the process of hearing is, therefore, more voluntary than in dialogues 1 and 2.

DIALOGUE 5

A: Hello, Kala. What a pleasant surprise!

B: Hello.

A: How have you been?

B: Not bad.

A: I heard you were abroad.

B: Yes, for a year. Now I'm back for good.

A: And how's Sudha? I hear she's got a scholarship.

B: Yes. She's leaving for the USA next month.

In dialogue 5 the word 'hear' has a different meaning: 'to be told about something'. It has little to do with the meaning of 'hear' in the first four dialogues, which is, the meaning we are concerned with for the present.

From some of the meanings of 'hear' that are relevant to language teaching and language learning, let us now move on to contexts in which 'listen' is used. As we shall see, listening is much more voluntary than hearing. When we listen to somebody or something, we pay special attention to what we can hear at any given time. Let us look at some contexts in which we listen to somebody or something.

DIALOGUE 6

A: Shanti, have you handed in your report? Tomorrow's the deadline.

B: Hmm? I'm going shopping. D'you need anything?

A: Shanti…are you listening? You've got to hand in your report tomorrow.

B: Sorry, I wasn't really listening. I'd forgotten I had a deadline to meet. Thanks for reminding me.

A: It might be a good idea to postpone your shopping.

B: I must, if I want to submit my report on time.

DIALOGUE 7

A: What've you got there?

B: These are CDs of Hariprasad Chaurasia's flute recitals.

A: How lovely! Of all the musical instruments I like the flute the most.

B: Would you like to listen to them?

A: I'd love to. Thanks.

In dialogue 6, speaker A asks speaker B to pay attention to what she/he is saying, that is, to the general content rather some specific portion of the content. In dialogue 7, B asks A if he/she would like to listen *to* the flute. Here listening does not necessarily require the listener to listen *for* specific information. Thus, listening to music for example, is a more general activity than listening to what someone says to you.

DIALOGUE 8

A: What a beautiful house you have!

B: I'm glad you like it. Would you like to go round and see the garden?

A: I'd enjoy that. (A and B go into the garden.)

B: Be prepared for a …

A: Sh, sh! Listen! Isn't that a dove cooing?

B: Yes, it is . It lives in the mango tree over there.

Here again B is asked to listen *to* something, namely listen *for* some specific information.

Dialogue 9

A: I see you're very busy.

B: Yes. I'm writing a tapescript.

A: What for?

B: To give the students practice in distinguishing between one consonant and another.

A: And how would you do that?

B: I would, for example, give them pairs of words like 'shine' and 'sign', which differ in respect of one sound only. Then the teacher says one of each pair of words, and the student ticks the right word.

A: So, this would help them distinguish between *s* and *sh*?

B: Yes. That's the idea.

In dialogue 9, speaker A listens carefully and is able to identify the sounds in the pair of words that speaker B gives as an example. Later, students will also have to pay attention to the teacher in order to identify the word the teacher says aloud.

Dialogue 10

A: What's this story for?

B: An exercise in listening.

A: And how d'you propose to use it?

B: At first the students will be asked to listen for the main events in the story.

A: And then?

B: Then they will listen for the words used to describe the main character and note them down.

A: They're sure to enjoy that.

In dialogue 10, the students will be expected to listen to the story as a whole and then listen for specific detail.

Thus, when we listen to music or the chirping of birds, for example, we pay attention in order to enjoy the particular experience as a whole. When on the other hand we listen for something we actually pay attention to detail and focus on specific information. It is mostly this intensive, focused listening that we concentrate on when we train students to listen in the classroom.

Activity 1 (Pair work)

Write dialogues in other contexts where the word 'hear' has the same meaning as in dialogues 1 to 4.

Activity 2 (Pair work)

Using dialogues 6 to 10 as examples, write at least one dialogue in which listening is general and one dialogue in which listening is more specific.

Functions of listening

We have so far seen that for teaching purposes, 'listening' generally happens as a much more deliberately focused activity than it does outside the classroom. Since it is deliberate, we have to ask ourselves why we listen and what we listen for in our daily lives. Answers to these two questions would help us arrive at some of the functions of listening, which in turn would determine the kinds of listening input we need to enable our students to become good listeners.

Activity 3 (Groups of 4)

Answer the following questions:
a. Why do we listen?
b. What is the main purpose of listening?
Then on the basis of your answers, discuss what some of the functions of listening are or what we listen for. List the functions agreed upon by the group and add them to the ones below.

Some Functions

1. We listen for the following kinds of information:
   a. General information to get an overall picture, derive the main idea
   b. Factual information, which can be selective or specific
   c. Detailed information, using which we draw inferences
2. We listen to find out more about spoken language, that is its distinctive features—namely pronunciation, vocabulary, and grammar and usage—features that distinguish it from written language.
3. We listen for pleasure to jingles, rhymes, numbers, short stories, anecdotes, etc.

Notice that listening helps us increase our knowledge of the world and our knowledge of the way language functions. As an aid to the development of our language skills it is indispensable and hence its importance in language teaching and learning. In the units that follow we shall concentrate on the process of listening and try to understand it as useful input to language learning.

Unit 2

Listing for the Main Idea or the Message

As discussed earlier, the main purpose of listening is to add to our existing knowledge of the world as well as our knowledge of language in general and of the spoken idiom in particular. In order to achieve this, we listen for information that can be general, factual or detailed. We also listen for spoken language. When we teach listening, therefore, it is necessary for us to focus our attention on:

a. The kinds of material we can use as input for a particular purpose and
b. The process, which can help us derive maximum benefit from what we listen to.

In this unit, we shall use some authentic material to understand the process of listening through which we arrive at the main idea or the message.

Activity 1 (Pair work)

a. Listen carefully to a short TV news report. Make a note of the words and expressions used, the introductory sentence, etc. which would help you to find out what the report is about.
b. Listen to the report again, and write down the message conveyed in one sentence. Discuss it with your partner in order to find out whether she/he agrees with you about what the report conveys.

ACTIVITY 2 (GROUPS OF 4)

a. Take turns to read out the sentences in which you summed up what the report was about. Tell the other members of the group how you arrived at the main idea and explain what technique(s) you used during the process of listening. For example, you may have been helped by clues like the ones in the figure below.

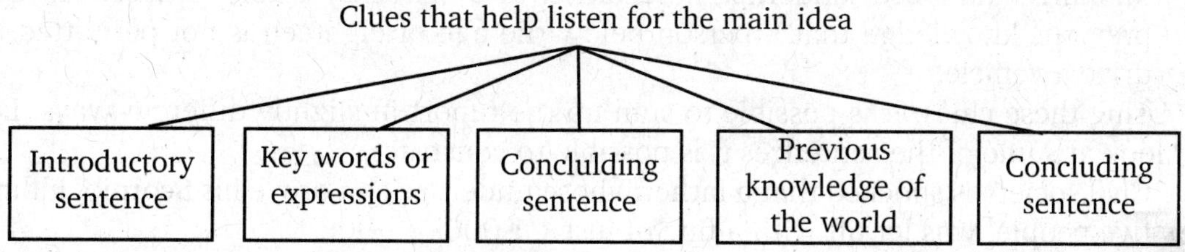

The introductory sentence in the report you listened to has the phrase 'hit-and-run case', which prepares you for what is to follow—an incident of a car driver hitting someone and not stopping to help. Some other key words and phrases that help you understand the main idea of the report are:

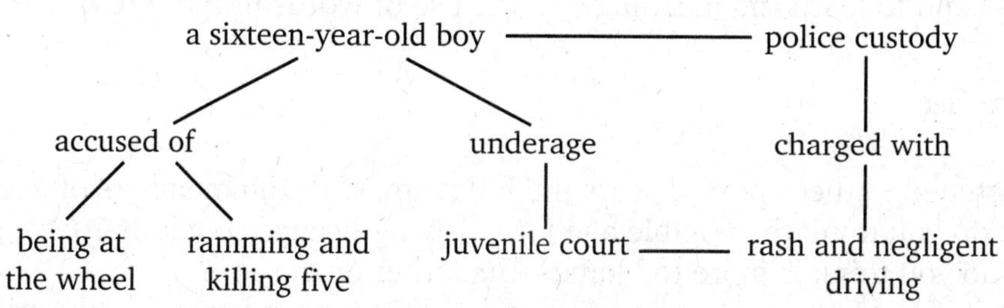

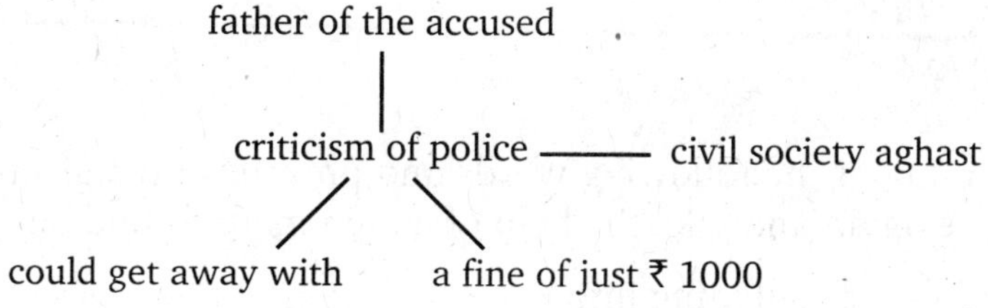

Notice:

a. that the words and phrases that are likely to attract our attention by and large comprise content words, that is, those words that are important for meaning, or nouns, main verbs, adjectives and adverbs.

b. that these words are perceived in relation to one another. It is their relatedness that makes us aware of the vocabulary used in connection with the offence: underage driving, its consequences; loss of life, and the punishment—fine, observation home, etc.
c. that in addition to these clues, we also use our previous knowledge to help us understand the message. For example, most of us have often heard the expression 'hit-and-run' used for drivers who run away after knocking down pedestrians. Similarly, the word 'underage' in relation to a sixteen-year-old is based on our previous knowledge that a person below the age of eighteen is not permitted to drive a vehicle.

Using these clues, it is possible to sum up the report in slightly different ways. Let us look at some of the sentences it is possible to construct.

– Civil society is shocked that a father whose underage son drove his Scorpio, killing five people, was let off with a fine of just ₹ 1,000.
– People are shocked that the police let the father of a sixteen-year-old at the wheel of his car that killed five people get away with a fine of just ₹ 1,000.
– It is shocking that the police took little or no action against a father whose sixteen-year-old son drove his Scorpio and killed five people.

Similarly, you could construct more sentences to convey the message of the report in different ways.

Next, engage in the following activities in pairs and groups to talk about what you listened to and to learn the meaning and the use of words in the report.

Activity 3 (Groups of 4)

Having listened to the report, discuss the following with the members of your group.

a. What do you think the eligible age for a driving licence should be? Give reasons.
b. Who do you think is more to blame—the father or the son?
c. Do you think the punishment (a fine of ₹ 1,000) is proportional to the crime? Give reasons for your answer.

Activity 4 (Pair work)

What is the meaning of the following words and phrases in the given context? Listen to the report once again and take the help of a dictionary to find out.

a. inconsolable
b. juvenile
c. culpable homicide
d. frustration
e. convicted
f. ramming into
g. let off
h. crack down
i. at the wheel
j. charged for (? with)
k. get away with

Notice that in the phrase 'charged for', the word 'for' has a question mark against it. The phrase should be 'charged with.' The reporter has made a mistake here probably because of the time constraint while reporting.

Activity 5 (Pair work)

Use these words and expressions in sentences of your own.

Now, listen to another dialogue on TV and pick out the word that tells you what is being discussed. Then engage in pairs and groups in activities that will help you listen efficiently.

Activity 6 (Groups of 4)

Listen to what the main speaker says, and while you listen, look at the following words and expressions. They are clues that will help you to make sense of what the speaker conveys.

environment(al), focus, degradation, development, balanced out, pollution, air, water, noise, put in place, impact assessments, projects, execution, urban areas, scrutiny, present, absent, comprehensive policy, ensure

Activity 7 (Groups of 4)

Write down the message conveyed in one or two sentences. You could write as many slightly different sentences as you wish to convey the main idea. For example, one possible summing up of the dialogue would be: 'In order to ensure that development takes place and that, at the same time, the environment is preserved, we need a national policy for the scrutiny of large projects.'

Activity 8

Each group can then share with the other groups the process they followed to arrive at the main idea discussed in the dialogue. The first step, for example would be to listen for the introductory sentence, which sets the tone for what follows.

Activity 9

Now look at the list of words and expressions provided as clues in Activity 6. Listen to the speaker once again and arrange them so as to indicate their relationship in terms

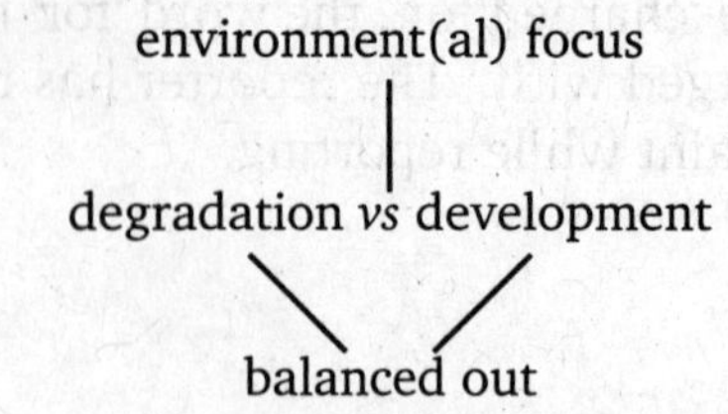

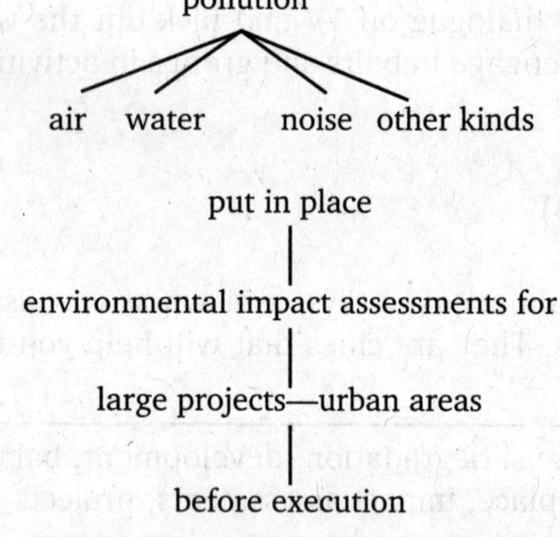

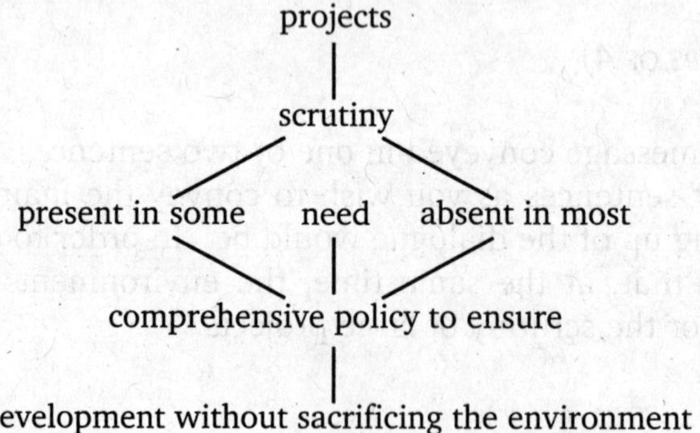

of what the dialogue conveys. One way of re-constructing the relationship is given below.

Activity 10 (Group Work)

In the next set of activities, you will talk within your group and with other groups about what you have listened to. Working with the members of your group, make a final statement of what you have listened to. One member from each group can then tell the other groups what they have summed up.

Activity 11 (Group work)

Each member of a group must suggest at least two ways in which the government can ensure that development does not happen at the cost of the environment. Other members of the group are free to express their agreement/disagreement to the suggestions.

To make suggestions, you could use any of the following expressions:

I think the government needs to ...
It might be a good idea for the government to ...
Maybe the government could ...
I suggest we help ...
I propose we ...
Why doesn't the government ...

To express agreement to a suggestion, you could use any of the following expressions:

I think you have a point ...
That's a very good idea ...
That should help ...
That'd be the best thing to do ...

To express disagreement to a suggestion, you could use any of the following expressions:

I don't think the government needs to ...
That's not a very good idea.
That would not be necessary.
It won't be worthwhile for the government.

Activity 12 (Group Work)

A representative of each group will present the suggestions that all the members of the group have agreed to.

Here are some points related to the activities you engaged in for you to ponder on with the members of your group.

ACTIVITY 13 (GROUPS OF 4)

Discuss the following questions and find the best answers to them.

a. What was the main aim of the listening activities?
b. Were the two recordings of television programmes clear and easy to understand?
c. How many times did you need to listen to the recordings? Did listening to them more than once help you to sum up the content?
d. Were the clues provided useful in the process of arriving at the gist of what you listened to?
e. Was the language of the news report and the dialogue on the environment very difficult/difficult/not so difficult/easy?
f. Were the news report and the dialogue too long/long/just right for the purpose for which they were intended?
g. Would you suggest any other kind of help that will be useful for your students to understand what they listen to?
h. Besides television programmes, what other sources would you draw upon for listening?

Bearing these questions in mind, look at the poem titled 'I Walk' in Appendix 5, that could be used to teach students of class 2 or 3 to listen for the main message.

ACTIVITY 14 (GROUPS OF 4)

Having looked at the poem and the activities designed to help students understand it, consider the following questions.

a. Do you think the prescribed 'English Reader' or textbook can be a useful resource for teaching listening?
b. Would the clues provided help your students understand the poem?
c. Can you suggest activities in addition to the ones given in Appendix 5 to help your students?
d. In addition to understanding the main message, what would students incidentally learn?
   For example: (i) They would learn to follow instructions.
   (ii) They would learn to appreciate rhyme.
e. Which level (in your institution) would this listening exercise be suitable for?

ACTIVITY 15 (GROUP WORK)

A representative from each group will then present its answers/point of view to the questions above.

Activity 16 (Groups of 4)

a. Look at a similar poem in Appendix 5 titled 'Frogs at School' which could be used to teach listening for the message or the theme at the same level, and design activities for groups of four students. You could begin by putting up the key words, and phrases (for example, 'school', 'be in time', and 'first . . . study') on the blackboard, and then read out or play a recording of the poem.
b. Look for those features of English that the student could incidentally learn from this poem apart from the main message. (for example, counting, sequence words, like 'first', and 'second', rhyme, 'doing' words, tense, and irregular verbs 'go' and 'went'.
c. Also look at the dialogue in Appendix 5 intended to teach listening to students at a higher level.

To sum up, we have seen:

1. that some materials we could use to train students to listen for the gist/main idea/ subject matter of what is said are:
   a. news reports, panel discussions, interviews on the TV/radio
   b. extracts from the prescribed textbook, for example poems, anecdotes, parts of stories and dialogues
2. that the materials we select for this purpose need to be short, or of no more than two minutes duration.
3. that the subject matter for listening depends on the level of the learners it is intended for. For example, short poems, conversations on animals, on the surroundings, anecdotes would be of interest to students of classes 1 to 4. Students of classes 5 to 8 would probably be interested in features on geography, travel, news, weather reports, sports and games. High school students could listen to interviews and talks/discussions on topics of current interest—the environment, space travel, scientific discoveries, travel, art, film and music. They would be interested in accounts of/discussion on topics relating to their subjects of study, for example history, science, economics, mathematics, geography. For purposes of listening, materials could be drawn from their prescribed texts and adapted.
4. that the technique used to teach listening for the main message is to prepare the student for what they are going to listen to by providing them with clues (key words). Clues help the learner to arrive at the message because these are generally content words (words that are important for meaning).
5. that the student needs to be encouraged to listen to the tape/CD more than once.
6. that to ensure understanding, listening activities must necessarily be related to and accompanied by speaking activities, such as repetition, role-play, and discussion in pairs and groups.

Unit 3

Listening for Factual Information

Very often in real-life situations, we have to listen for facts that we are required to record for various purposes in our professional lives, for example at meetings. On a personal level too we may have to record factual information about a whole range of subjects, for example shows, holidays, places to see and flats on rent or sale, in order to select what we find most suitable or attractive. Keeping in view these general purposes for which we are likely to listen for factual information, therefore, we consider two types of material that could be used to teach listening.

Activity 1

Listen carefully to the facts about the sales of the two daily newspapers. Plot them on the chart below and draw a graph of the number of daily newspapers circulated over a period of six months (January to June) to find out which of the two papers is more widely circulated and more popular. Also, find out whether the sales of the two papers increased, decreased or remained steady over the six-month period.

	January	February	March	April	May	June
1000						
950						
900						
850						
800						
750						
700						
650						
600						
550						
500						
450						
400						
350						
300						
250						
200						
150						
100						
50						
10						

Activity 2 (Groups of 4)

Now from the graph that you have prepared, tell the members of your group how many copies of the paper were sold each month from January to June.

Activity 3 (Groups of 4)

Compare the sale of each paper every month. (Use comparatives such as 'larger than', 'not as many…as…', 'smaller than', 'more than', 'far greater than', etc.)

Activity 4 (Groups of 4)

Of the three main newspapers sold in your state, which one do you think has the largest circulation. Give reasons. Tell the members of your group which newspaper you read and why. (Compare the newspaper you read with other papers that you think are not as good as the one you read in terms of the focus, content, language, photography, reliability, etc.) If other members of your group disagree with you, be prepared to defend your choice of newspaper.

Activity 5

If you agree with other members of your group with regard to their choice of paper and the reasons for their choice, respond using any of the following expressions: 'yes', 'you're right', 'quite right', 'absolutely', 'yes, it is', 'I agree', 'I think so too'.

If you disagree with their choice, tell them your reasons for doing so. To do this, begin by using any of the following expressions: 'it certainly isn't…', 'I don't think so', 'I don't agree', 'that's not true' or 'but it can't be…'.

Now listen for information on an entirely different subject—planning a holiday. You wish to go on holiday, but you cannot make up your mind about the places you would like to visit. An advertisement on television offering a truly perfect vacation gives you information about package tours to some beautiful places at a discount.

Activity 6

Listen to the information carefully and as you listen fill in the details in the chart below. This will probably help you decide where you want to go on holiday.

S. No.	Tour package	Places	Duration of tour	Places to stay	Charges from starting point

Activity 7 (Groups of 4 – 6)

Look at the information on your chart and decide which place you would like to go to. Then you must tell the other members of the group why you chose to take a particular tour. (Possible considerations for the choice could be duration of tour, cost of tour, approximate cost of meals other than breakfast, other incidental expenditure, fare to the starting point of tour, their budget, value for money spent, etc.)

Activity 8 (Groups of 4 – 6)

Regroup according to your choice of the tour. A group representative will tell the other groups why the members of his/her group selected that particular tour package.

Activity 9 (Groups of 4 – 6)

Seek clarifications regarding the tour your group would like to take. List all the questions you wish to ask Crystal Travel and Tours before making a final decision (for example, questions about dates of tours, rail/air fare to starting point and back, transport, sightseeing spots, shopping and special discount for group tours).

Activity 10 (Groups of 4 – 6)

Share the questions the members of your group would like to ask the travel agency with the other groups. The groups add questions they may have missed.

Activity 11 (Groups of 4 – 6)

Discuss the following points about the subskill listening for factual information and how training students in this can enhance their learing of English.

a. Can you think of at least three types of information we need to listen for in real-life situations (in the classroom, at home, in public life, at the work place, etc.)?
b. The types of information we gather through listening are closely related to the purposes for which we use the information. Can you think of at least three purposes which information we get through listening could serve (for example, data collection, general knowledge, pleasure or travel)? Give examples of the kind of input we could give students to help them listen for information with respect to some of the purposes you have listed.

c. Do you think listening for information can be a useful language learning tool? If yes, then can you think of what (context-related language, for example) a student of English can learn from the type of information he listens for?
d. What types of activities would help a student to acquire context-related language? (for example, listening to instructions→carrying them out→giving instructions).
e. Think of a listening activity that could help your class learn the language used in a particular context. While doing so, remember that the listening exercise must be suitable for the level of students you have in mind.

UNIT
4

LISTENING FOR DETAIL

When we listen to a talk or a lecture on a topic of interest, we would like to remember the details. This is not easy unless we are able to record what we have listened to in some way Doing this will help us reconstruct the information and refer to it for the discussion that follows a talk, or retrieve the information at a later date when we require it. In this unit, we will see how developing the art of notetaking is necessary to this end.

Understanding the subskill

You will listen to part of a programme telecast by CNBC and note down details about the panellists and what some of them have to say.

ACTIVITY 1

Listen carefully to the anchor's* introduction to the programme. Give the programme a title.

* a person who introduces and guides a programme through its various stages

ACTIVITY 2

Take down the details of the five panellists whom the anchor introduces under the following headings.

panellist's name	profession	area of specialisation	designation

ACTIVITY 3

Note down the anchor's question and the points the second panellist makes in response.

When you take down notes, make sure you do not write complete sentences. Remember that in order to keep pace with the speaker you should take down only the main points and the key words, using conventional as well as your own abbreviations. Some standard abbreviations are:

e.g. : example
etc. : etcetera
∴ : therefore
∵ : because
i.e. : that is
c.f. : compare
vs : versus

Some 'invented' abbreviations, for example, could be:

imp : important
int'l : international
pts : points
= : equal to

You can invent many such others while you are listening. Finally, you could start taking notes like this:

Indian Constitution → freedom of religion
Freedom to be govnd by pers(onal) law
Hindu family → Hindu Succn Act → daughter's share = son's

ACTIVITY 4 (GROUPS OF 4)

Listen to Shobha again and try to guess the meanings of the following words from the context.

personal laws
co-parcenary property

amendment
bequeathed
testator
disinherit

If you are not able to guess the meanings, consult a dictionary.

Activity 5 (Groups of 4)

Now use your notes to reconstruct what Shobha said and discuss the points she made.

Activity 6 (Groups of 4)

Group representatives will write on the blackboard the points they have noted down. Add points that your group may have missed. Discuss the following questions in your group.

a. Does the Hindu Succession Act guarantee complete equality between a daughter and a son? (What does 'equal share' under the Hindu Succession Act refer to?)
b. Is the equal right to individual property foolproof? Why or why not? (For example, how can a woman be deprived of this right differentially under Hindu law and Muslim law?)
c. Do you think the law should ensure that a woman gets an equal share of property irrespective of whether it is individual property or joint property? If yes, suggest ways in which this can be done. Present your views to the other groups.

Activity 7

Listen carefully to the anchor's questions to Purvi. Make a note of the inheritance rights that an adopted child may have if she fulfils certain conditions. What are those conditions? While listening, look at the questions below. They will help you listen for these details.

a. Can we adopt two children of the same sex?
b. Can they be adopted under the same law?
c. Do both have full inheritance rights?
d. What can we do to protect the inheritance rights of the second child?

Activity 8 (Groups of 4)

Listen to Shobha's answers to the following questions and then discuss the following. After you finish, present your views and experiences to the other groups.

a. What happens when a will is contested?
b. What are the ingredients of a valid will?
c. Can a valid will always prevent a son from contesting it? Can you cite instances you know of or you think are possible when the son has challenged/can challenge the will even though it is valid? (For example, the will could be challenged on the grounds that the two witnesses are partisan.)

ACTIVITY 9 (GROUPS OF 4)

Do you know any instances when the court has upheld a valid will that has been challenged? Tell the members of your group about this.

ACTIVITY 10 (GROUPS OF 4)

Listen to the last part of the discussion and consider the following questions with the members of your group. After you finish, present your answers to the other groups.

a. The anchor asks Shobha, 'Have you come across any instances when people are not getting maintenance and support from their husbands?' What does she mean by 'maintenance and support'? (The meaning becomes clear from what the panellist says in response to the anchor.)
b. Does she get an answer to her question?
c. Why does a panellist want to know if there is any provision besides what is in the letter of law that can 'enforce that a person has full right …'? (Perhaps it is because of the problem she mentions.)
d. Does she receive an answer?
e. What does the anchor confine the discussion of women's rights to?
f. What is Rani's answer?

ACTIVITY 11 (GROUPS OF 4)

Can you suggest at least two ways (other than legal provisions) of ensuring that men and women have equal rights? You could give instances where these have worked/not worked.

ACTIVITY 12 (GROUPS OF 4)

Listen to the discussion again and make a note of the speakers' hesitations during their explanation of legal and social issues. What marks their hesitations? Why do they pause or use fillers while they speak? (For example, do these tell you something about the nature of spoken language? Is it different from written English?) Share your thoughts with the other groups.

Points to ponder

a. In addition to obtaining information on women's rights (which is part of the panel discussion) think of what you have learnt incidentally in the process of listening to the discussion and participating in the activities. (Looking at activities 10, 11 and 12 will help you understand this better.)
b. Based on the panel discussion, think of other activities you could add to the existing ones. (Choose those activities that the programme lends itself to.)
c. In this unit, you saw how a television programme could form the basis for the listening activities. Think of recent programmes that you have watched. Of these, which ones do you feel would be suitable for your class? Why do you think so?
d. Apart from television programmes think of other types of listening materials suitable for your students to listen to for information. (You could consider the possibility of using other subjects of study, for example, history, geography, etc. in addition to extracts from their English textbooks.

Let us sum up

a. We generally listen to discussions/lectures for information about some subject/issue either because it is of general interest and is socially significant or because it adds to our knowledge of the subject or provides us with entirely new information.
b. If you take down notes whenever you listen to a subject of interest to you, it might be a good idea to develop your own set of abbreviations. Thus, we have listened to part of a panel discussion on women's rights and used abbreviations to note down details. Some of the abbreviations are conventional, while others are invented.
c. From our notes, we reconstructed (in parts) the discussion on women's rights.
d. We familiarised ourselves with the vocabulary relating to women's legal entitlement.
e. We followed the actual conduct of the discussion from the points of view of the anchor and the panellists. In addition to noting the facts, we extended the subject of women's rights to related discussions, which included our experience and knowledge of a woman's world.
f. We considered other television programmes that we think might be suitable for teaching our students listening.
g. We saw that, in addition to using television or radio programmes for teaching listening, it is possible to use other resources.
h. We listened for features that are characteristic of spoken English and considered the general nature of spoken language vis-à-vis written language.

Teaching the subskill

Having considered the possibility of using listening materials other than television programmes for your students, look at the transcript of a story given in Appendix 5 intended for school children of classes 5 and 6. Let us design activities that will help students listen for the facts in the story and also draw inferences from them.

Activity 1

Listen to the story carefully and give it a title. (Clue: The word *golden* occurs several times in the story.)

Activity 2

Listen carefully to the story again for answers to the following questions.

a. Who was Raju?
b. Why did the king reward Raju?
c. What was his reward?
d. What did the king ask Raju to do?

Activity 3

Listen to the story again and, while you listen, fill in the blank spaces in the following sentences.

a. People called the stream the Golden River because ....
b. Early one morning before .... Raju took his net and ....
c. Raju said to himself, 'I must catch plenty of fish this morning. If I don't ....'
d. Raju wanted to go home, but just then ....
e. Raju pulled the net to the bank and found ....
f. ...., the fish spoke to him.
g. The fish said, 'Please ....'
h. The fish shone .... It was ....
i. He felt ....
j. He took it carefully out of the net and ....
k. .... an old man came slowly along the river path and ....
l. '..........................?' he asked.
m. '..........................' said Raju.
n. 'Sit by the fire and eat with us. ....'
o. 'In the morning, ...'
p. But the old man had ....

q. The next morning, Raju took .... He felt weak because ....
r. Inside was ....
s. 'But, if I throw you into the river, ...' cried Raju.
t. Raju looked at the beautiful fish, and he felt sad. 'I can't ....,' he thought.
u. He saw some men ....
v. Under the umbrella ....
w. Behind him ....
x. 'I was the old man, and .... I was the ...., and you ....'
y. 'You were .... Now, I want to .... Please come ....'
z. He lived there ....

Activity 4 (Groups of 5)

Discuss the following questions in your group and agree upon answers to them. A representative from your group will then present your point of view.

a. Is the story you have just listened to a true story?
b. How do we know that the fish is not an ordinary fish? Why does the king become a fish and then an old man?
c. Does the story convey any message? If it does, then what is the message?

Activity 5

If you were in Raju's place, would you act in the same way?
You could answer in the following ways:

If I were in Raju's place I would/would not do what he did because ....

OR

If I were in Raju's place, I would not be able to decide what to do because ....

Activity 6 (Groups of 5)

Choose any three of the following situations and tell your group:

a. what you would do if you won a lottery.
b. what you would do if your friend asked you to help them do their homework.

c. what you would do if you found a wallet/purse in the playground in your school.
d. what you would do if your neighbours were noisy at night.
e. what you would do if you had a bad headache.

For example, if you were talking about the first situation, you could begin with: 'If I won a lottery I would . . . ,' and complete your statement with any one or two of the following options or any other of your choice.

- give all the money to my parents
- buy my family a flat
- help some of my friends who have very little money
- donate some of the money to an orphanage
- put away (some of) the money for a rainy day
- request my parents to take care of my money for me

Unit 5

Listening as an Aid to Learning about Spoken English

In this unit, we shall listen to a few dialogues and pay special attention to the features that are characteristic of spoken language. You will notice that the English that people use in conversation, particularly informal conversation, is slightly different from the English we are used to reading in books. For convenience, we could start with the smallest unit of speech, that is, sounds.

Listening for sounds

Activity 1

Before you listen to the conversations on the CD, consider the following questions.

a. Are the sounds in English the same as the letters of the alphabet?
b. Can you think of words in which the sounds and the letters do not match?
c. Do you find any of the sounds of English difficult to produce?
d. Can you think of at least one reason why you find the sounds difficult to produce?

Activity 2 (Groups of 4)

Listen carefully to dialogues 1, 2 and 3. Pick out words in which the spellings do not match their pronunciations. For example, in the word *bridge* in dialogue 1, the letter 'd' is not pronounced. Also, the 'j' in *joking*, the 'g' in *danger* and the 'dg' in *bridge* represent the same consonant sound, that is, the first sound in the word *jar*.

In the word *cross*, the letter 'o' represents the vowel sound in *hot*, but in the word *flowing*, it represents the vowel sound in the word *go*, and in the word *above*, it represents the vowel sound in the word *hut*. Dialogues 1 and 2 have been transcribed for you to illustrate the correspondence between the letters and the sounds of English. (refer to Appendix 2).

Activity 3 (Groups of 4)

After you have listed examples of the mismatch between spellings and sounds, make a list of the kinds of mismatch. Add your own examples to the ones you have picked from the dialogues. Representatives from each group will write examples of mismatch between spellings and sounds and classify these under types.

Activity 4 (Groups of 4)

Listen to the dialogues again and pick out the consonant sounds that you find difficult to produce. Give more examples of words in which those sounds occur. Do you find it difficult to distinguish between one consonant sound and another? Write down a pair of words for each pair of sounds you find difficult. For example, if you find it difficult to distinguish between the first sounds in the words ***z**oo* and ***J**ew*, then write down another pair of words which have the same sounds, for example *sei**z**e* and *sie**g**e*.

Activity 5

Listen once more to the dialogues and make a note of the vowel sounds that you find difficult to produce. If you find it difficult to produce a vowel sound, for example that in the word *straight*, give examples of words in which the sound occurs. If you find it difficult to distinguish between one vowel sound and another, think of pairs of words that differ only in the two sounds. Try saying the pairs of words. For example, another pair of words to distinguish between the vowels in the words *f**a**te* and *f**igh**t* would be *s**a**ne* and *s**ig**n*.

Note: For practice in consonant and vowel sounds that you find difficult, refer to the materials in Appendix 3.

Listening for stressed syllables and words

In this section we shall listen to the dialogues for words that prominently heard and also locate the most prominent syllable in those words.

Activity 6 (Groups of 4)

Listen to the conversations carefully and read their transcripts. Underline those words that sound prominent in each utterance. For example, in A's utterance in the first conversation, the words *cross, bridge, quickly, can* are said louder and sound more prominent than the other words in that utterance. After you have finished, compare your answers with those of the other groups.

Activity 7

Identify the categories of words you have underlined as prominent. For example, in dialogue 1, the word *cross* is a verb, *bridge* is a noun, *quickly* is an adverb.

You must have noticed that the categories of words that are generally stressed in conversation are those that are important for the meaning of an utterance and those that are generally weak or unstressed are not important for the meaning of an utterance.

When words that are important for meaning have more than one vowel sound, they are said to have more than one syllable. There are, in other words, as many syllables in a word as there are vowel sounds. In words with more than one syllable, only one of them is stressed. Thus, in the word *quickly*, there are two vowel sounds and hence two syllables. Of these, the first syllable *qui* receives the stress*.

Activity 8 (Groups of 4)

Each group listens to 2, 11 and 12 dialogues for the stress on the words underlined in the transcript in Appendix 2. Use a vertical stroke above and in front of the stressed syllable of a word, as in *'quickly, 'confident, 'bridge***.

---

* Though words of one syllable are not marked for stress in the dictionary, here they do have the mark to indicate that in connected speech they are stressed.

** For more information on word and sentence stress, refer to p. 100, Appendix 3.

ACTIVITY 9 (GROUPS OF 4)

A representative of each group then tells the other groups which syllable in the underlined words in the dialogues is stressed. You could write the words on the blackboard and then mark stress. Also point out the category of words that have generally been stressed, for example nouns, adjectives, etc. There may sometimes be exceptions to the general rule, for example words that are normally stressed may not be stressed in some contexts.

ACTIVITY 10 (GROUPS OF 4)

a. Listen carefully to the words *has*, *have* and *had* in dialogues 10, 11 and 12. You will notice that the meaning of the word in the context determines the stress. Can you pick out the context in which *has* has not been stressed? For example, when the word *has**** means to 'to possess', it is not stressed.
b. Now listen again to dialogue 12 for a word that is normally stressed but has not been stressed in the given context. Here is a clue to help you locate the word: a word repeated immediately after it has been uttered is not stressed.
c. From dialogue 12, can you pick out any other word that ought normally to be stressed but is not stressed?

In the next section we shall listen to the dialogues for words that have not been stressed.

Listening for unstressed words

ACTIVITY 11 (GROUPS OF 4)

a. Listen to any three dialogues carefully and note down the words that have not been stressed.
b. Compare notes with the other members of your group and list the unstressed words under the parts of speech (for example, pronouns, and articles) they belong to.
c. Group representatives will put up the categories of words that they heard as unstressed. Identify the parts of speech that are normally not stressed in spoken English.

*** The words *have/has/had* are stressed when they mean 'suffer from', or 'experience' or 'receive' and when they are attached to the short form of the negative *not* as in *haven't*.

ACTIVITY 12 (GROUPS OF 4)

Now listen to the dialogues once again and make a note of those words that have been stressed even though they belong to the category of words that are normally not stressed in connected speech. For example, the word *can* in A's utterance in dialogue 1 is a modal verb and is generally not stressed. But in this context, it occurs in the final position in A's utterance, and in that position, modal verbs are stressed. (Compare the utterance of *can* in dialogue 1 with the utterance of *can* in the medial position in other dialogues). Give other examples of words that are normally not stressed but have been stressed in the dialogues.

ACTIVITY 13 (GROUPS OF 4)

On the basis of lists of the parts of speech of words that are generally stressed your or unstressed in connected speech, frame a general rule that can help you to stress the right words when you speak.

Listening for colloquialisms*

ACTIVITY 14

Listen to dialogues 1–11 and make a note of words and expressions that you are not quite familiar with. Some of these may have different meanings in different contexts. Look up the meanings of these words and phrases in the dictionary. Listen to the conversations again and pay attention to the use of the following words/expressions, which, occur in the order in which they have been listed.

don't think so	get the project proposal
get on with	Oh, come on
Sorry?	you made it
don't get you	help yourself to
catch the 8 a.m.	work station
making time	flexi time
hopping mad	have the flu
get on the train	

* expressions or words used in informal conversation

Activity 15

Look at the words and phrases in column 1 and match them with their meanings in column 2.

Column 1	Column 2
a. don't think so	very angry
b. get on with	board
c. Sorry?	suffer from
d. don't get you	receive
e. catch the 8 a.m.	managed to reach/be present at
f. making time	know that what someone said is not true or right
g. hopping mad	work a fixed number of hours per day/week; start and finish work according to our choice
h. get on the train	cubicle in an office for an individual to work
i. get the project proposal	to take what you want
j. Oh, come on	making an effort to find time
k. you made it	not believe something is true
l. help yourself to	could you repeat what you said
m. work station	the train/bus leaving at 8 a.m.
n. flexi time	progress with one's work
o. have the flu	don't understand

Activity 16 (Groups of 4)

You must have noticed that the word *get* has been used in different contexts and, therefore, has different meanings. In conversation, there are many other words that are used quite often. For example, the verbs *make* and *do* combine with words to convey different meanings in varying contexts. First, look at some of the phrases that are generally used in conversation and look up a dictionary for their meanings.

a. *get*
   - i. get something (for yourself or for somebody)
   - ii. get a channel from a television or radio station
   - iii. get a newspaper, magazine
   - iv. get marks/a grade
   - v. get used to, angry, bored, etc.
   - vi. get to know
   - vii. get dirty
   - viii. get back

b. *make*
   i. make a will
   ii. make movies
   iii. make tea/coffee/breakfast/lunch
   iv. make do
   v. make something of your life
   vi. make off with something
   vii. make money

c. *do*
   i. do the flowers
   ii. do the soup
   iii. do the dishes
   iv. do without
   v. do somebody out of
   vi. do a sum or a crossword
   vii. do a trip/14 kilometres to a litre of petrol
   viii. do a drawing/painting
   viii. do history, geography. etc.

d. *go*
   i. go through something
   ii. go down (sun or moon; ship)
   iii. go by
   iv. go into
   v. go over something

e. *look*
   i. look into
   ii. look out for somebody
   iii. look somebody up
   iv. look through somebody
   v. look through something

Each member of the group must construct three contexts in each of which at least one of the phrases occurs. For example, look at a context in which the phrase 'look somebody up' occurs.

(A visits B in his office.)

A: Can I come in?

B: Yes. Oh what a pleasant surprise! How nice to see you. Where've you been all these years?

A: I was transferred to Kolkata. It was all very sudden.

B: No wonder! Are you still in Kolkata?

A: No. I'm back again. Just stopped by to say hello.

B: How thoughtful of you. We must meet again soon to catch up (on each other).

A: Yes, we must.

B: Do *look me up* when you have the time.

A: Certainly. If you'll excuse me, I must be going to the office now. Bye, bye!

B: Bye!

Activity 17 (Groups of 4)

Each group can enact one of the dialogues they have written.

Activity 18

Look at the phrases under a–e again. In column 1, write down each phrase and in column 2, write down the verb that would be used in its place in formal writing. Follow the examples given below.

Column 1	Column 2
get back	return
make movies	produce, direct or act in

Listening for contractions

In this section, we will listen to the dialogues for two words that have been combined to form one word. This shortening, or contraction, of words is characteristic of spoken English.

Your group listens to at least three dialogues and lists the words that have shortened forms. This happens when one of the two words is shortened and attached to another complete word. For example, listen for the words *don't* and *shouldn't* in dialogue 1. The first word is a combination of *do* and the shortened form of the negative *not*. Similarly, the word *shouldn't* is a combination of *should* and the shortened form of *not*. Group representatives will put up lists on the blackboard. Look at the lists and say what kinds of words generally combine in speech.

...ity 19 (Groups of 4)

...up listens to at least three dialogues and lists the words that have shortened ...s happens when one of the two words is shortened and attached to another ...ord. For example, listen for the words *don't* and *shouldn't* in dialogue 1.

The first word is a combination of *do* and the shortened form of the negative *not*. Similarly, the word *shouldn't* is a combination of *should* and the shortened form of *not*. Group representatives will put up lists on the blackboard. Look at the lists and say what kinds of words generally combine in speech.

Points to ponder

a. At what level would you use listening to teach pronunciation and spoken English?
b. What kinds of materials would you use to teach your class pronunciation and/or spoken English? (This could include instructions, stories told in class, imitation, etc.)
c. How much pronunciation would you teach your class?
d. What techniques would you use to help your students learn spoken English through listening? (For example, repetition, recitation, re-framing, etc.)

ACTIVITY 20 (GROUPS OF 4)

Discuss your thoughts on the points raised above with the others in your group. Your representative will then present the views of the group and give reasons for them.

ACTIVITY 21 (GROUPS 4)

Each group lists the characteristics of spoken English that they have learnt from the activities relating to the dialogues they have listened to. For example, from the first four activities we learnt that there is a mismatch between spelling and sound in English. In other words, we cannot tell how a word is pronounced from its spelling. The pronunciation of words has therefore to be learnt.

ACTIVITY 22

Each group then selects listening materials for their class (some materials are given in Appendix 2) and prepares activities to help their class listen to spoken English for any one feature of pronunciation and/or usage.
(The feature you select would depend upon the level of your students.)

Let us sum up

In this unit, we have focused on some of the characteristics of spoken English through listening. You must have noticed that:

a. the materials we have used for listening to features of spoken English are dialogues because they closely resemble the kind of oral interaction that normally takes place between people every day, and to that extent they are an authentic representation of spoken English.
b. each feature of spoken English has been considered under a separate section, so that we may concentrate on one feature at a time and listen to a dialogue for only that feature.
c. the dialogues do not always contain all the aspects of a particular feature, but are used to introduce a feature which is then explored through the activities. For example, the use of the verb *get* in the dialogues forms the basis for the introduction through activities of other verbs (for example, *do*, *make*, *go*, and *look*) commonly used in phrases. Note that it would be useful to get students to listen to these and other phrases in dialogues so as to enable them to understand how they are used.
d. the feature/s of spoken English we focus on would depend upon the students' level and their knowledge and experience.
e. enacting the dialogue can help internalise those features of speech that you have been focusing on.
f. listening to dialogues/conversations for features that characterise spoken English is intended to activate what you probably know already and is therefore awareness-raising rather than being entirely new information/knowledge.

Part II

Speaking

UNIT 6

THE NEED FOR SPEAKING

While it is absolutely necessary for students to master their mother tongue, or first language, which forms a critical part of their identity, the acquisition of the second language, English, is of paramount importance to them in functioning effectively both socially and academically as well as in pursuing their careers.

In order to be proficient in a language we need to acquire the four skills—listening, speaking, reading and writing. For a long time, the majority perception that only reading and writing skills had to be mastered influenced textbook construction/design/content in English. Gradually, with the continuing growth of telecommunications worldwide and the increasing importance of spoken communication in the context of globalisation, this perception of the learning of English as a second language underwent a revision to include listening and speaking skills.. We cannot over-emphasise the need to develop our aural-oral skills in addition to our reading and writing skills, for communication consists of all the four. One is tempted to ask why it is necessary to be able to speak well. For an answer to this question we would have to survey the academic, professional and social scenarios, (in India and the rest of the world) which our students are likely to function in.

There is no doubt that the majority of Indian students speak only their mother tongue at home and in their immediate social contexts. The only context in which many of them can get an opportunity to communicate in English is the English classroom. Hence training in the effective use of English must begin in school. We have to make maximal use of the classroom 'context' to simulate other contexts that students might in the future find themselves in. Let us consider these contexts.

Social contexts

An increase in inter-state mobility has led to an increase in the number of students migrating to other states for higher education. In the absence of a common Indian language to communicate in, they are compelled to use English. It then becomes the language they communicate in every day. Thus students in colleges/universities communicate in their mother tongue and also in English with other speakers of the same language, and in English in the classroom and with speakers of other languages. Later in their professions also students if they are not proficient in English are likely to encounter the problem of communicating with colleagues from other Indian states and sometimes from other parts of the world.

It is, therefore, necessary for us as teachers to design materials that provide students with ample opportunity to practise the use of English in various social contexts, such as meeting and greeting people, introducing themselves and others, inviting people to a get-together, a dance recital or a play, inquiring after a classmate's health and offering to help a classmate with studies, that would enable them to hone their oral communication skills in English.

Academic contexts

Besides knowing how to use English in social contexts, students require proficiency in the use of English in academic contexts. Those students for whom English is the medium of instruction need to acquire a high degree of proficiency in the language in order to understand and discuss topics related to the various subjects that they study. Materials in listening and speaking would be of immense help to these students if they are broad-based, that is, if they incorporate a variety of topics related to their subjects of study—nature study, geography, social studies, science, computers, etc. The advantage of incorporating these would be that students would understand and learn to use the vocabulary and structures while talking about these subjects in context. Not only would such materials enable students to speak English in the English classroom but also to express themselves clearly when they need to discuss the other subjects they study.

Students who have a regional language as the medium of instruction would require more help and, therefore, materials that are graded. Moving from easy activities to more difficult ones would be immensely useful. In addition to that in the English textbook, vocabulary and grammar relating to other subjects of study could be introduced *after* they have been encouraged to speak English.

ACTIVITY 1 (GROUPS OF 4)

Each member must make a list of the social contexts in which their students would need to speak English. Then the group makes a common list of these contexts and reads them out to the other groups. A volunteer from one of the groups writes a combined list on the blackboard.

Activity 2 (Groups of 4)

Each member can make a second list of the academic contexts their students would need to speak English in. The group writes down a list of these contexts. The groups discuss which of the contexts in the combined list are common to all the students and put them up on the blackboard.

Activity 3 (Groups of 4)

Can you think of any other contexts in which your students are likely to communicate in English? Tell the other groups what you think these are and why. Discuss this issue with the other groups, (all the teachers may not agree with your point of view) and arrive at a solution acceptable to the majority.

Identifying context-related language

When we consider different contexts, we have to remind ourselves that common to all of them is the relationship between the people who are speaking to each other. By this we mean that we interact with various people, some of whom are just acquaintances while others are good friends, colleagues or relatives. There are also people we meet for the first time on an official occasion. Very often the relationship between participants in an interaction determines the kind of language we use. For example, we would address a friend, a relative or a colleague by their first name, but a stranger, a boss, a teacher or an acquaintance by their titles. While the first form of address would be 'informal', the latter form of address would be 'formal'. Similarly, forms of greeting could be formal in the case of people we hardly know or people who are senior in age and position, but informal in the case of our friends, colleagues or relatives of our age. We would greet the former using 'Good morning', 'Good afternoon', 'Hello'. To greet friends, relatives our age, colleagues we would use 'Hi/Hello' (Sometimes along with first names). Also, the place and purpose of interaction determines the extent to which we can be formal/informal. In an academic discussion, for example, we would need to use English that is formal and socially appropriate. Similarly, for official transactions our language (vocabulary, grammar) would be formal. In day-to-day conversation, interaction, among friends, classmates and colleagues, on the other hand, the idiom would be informal/colloquial.

Theoretically speaking, there can be very fine distinctions along a formality–informality cline ranging from extremely formal to extremely informal. In practical terms, however, we as teachers would need to enable students to make a broad distinction between formal and informal. Finer distinctions are generally acquired at an advanced stage in the acquisition of a second language (here English).

In addition to the relationship between participants in a conversation (formal/informal), an awareness of the following is necessary for successful communication to take place:

1. socio-cultural norms (politeness, impoliteness, differences in meanings of words that are common to two varieties of a language)
2. meanings of words and their use in context
3. the correct grammatical form of an utterance.

In other words, an awareness of these minimises chances of misunderstanding. Let us look at the effect that the inappropriate use of English can have on oral communication.

Activity 1

Listen to and read the following conversations and anecdote and identify inappropriate expressions, vocabulary or grammar in each.

a. Ms Sinha: Latif, could you send Jacob and Gita upstairs?
Mr Kapadia: Yes. I'll shunt them upstairs straightaway.

b. Seema: Hello, when did you get back?
Mr Rao: (Hello.) This morning.
Seema: I'm sorry to hear that your son met with an accident.
Mr Rao: It's all right.

c. Sunil: You look very pretty in this dress.
Sunita: Thank you.
Sunil: You're welcome.

d. Sangeeta: You seem to be hot and bothered. Can I get you a drink?
Nishanth: A cup of (black) coffee, if it's not too much trouble.
Sangeeta: Not at all. It won't take me more than a minute. I have the concoction ready.
Nishanth: Thanks.

e. Gargi: Did you see the advertisement in the papers?
Farhan: D'you mean the ad for teaching posts in Central University?
Gargi: Yes. There are nine vacancies for the post of Associate Professor. Why don't you apply for it?
Farhan: No, I can't. I'm not illegible for the post.

f. Ms Rao: You didn't attend the meeting yesterday. Anything the matter?
Mr Kumar: No. I was not knowing there was a meeting.

g. Akanksha: Can I be of any help.

Ramesh: No. I don't need your help. I've got ten people to do the job.

h. Sheetal (*Peeps into Ganesh's office.*): Excuse me....

Kalyan: What d'you want?

Sheetal: Nothing. I'm looking for Gita. It's urgent.

Kalyan: Well, Gita's not here.

i. Teacher: Have you read Aesop's fables?

Student: Yes. I'm reading them during the vacation.

j. (*Nisha is at home. The phone rings.*)

Nisha: Hello.

Jacob: Can I speak to Ms Nisha Thakur?

Nisha: Speaking.

Jacob: I'm Jacob from the fourth floor.

Nisha: Sorry? The fourth floor? Which fourth floor?

Jacob: From OCS.

Nisha: Er....mm.

Jacob: From Orient Consultancy Services.

Nisha: Oh dear! I thought it was someone from the fourth floor of one of the flats here.

Jacob: I should have said I'm from Orient Consultancy Services to begin with.

Nisha: Yes?

Jacob: Madam, we are having a get-together at the Boat Club at 7.30 p.m. tomorrow. Please do come.

Nisha: What's the occasion?

Jacob: It's the annual get-together.

Nisha: I see. Thank you, Jacob.

Jacob: Bye, bye, Madam.

Nisha: Bye, Jacob, and thanks again.

k. An Englishman went to visit a friend who owned a large fruit-growing estate in Jamaica. Greatly impressed by the enormous quantity of fruit he saw and realising that it was too perishable to be exported when ripe, he exclaimed: 'But what do you do with all this fruit? You surely can't eat it all yourselves.' 'Oh,' replied his friend, taking advantage of his familiarity with American usage to make a pun, 'We eat what we can, and we can what we can't.' This greatly amused the Englishman, who resolved to remember it for the benefit of his friends at home.

Shortly after his return to England, he attended a dinner, at which he was asked to give his impressions of Jamaica. He did so, and decided to use his friend's joke as a climax to his speech. So after recounting his experience he added, 'My friend made a rather neat pun while he was showing me round his estate. I was struck by the large amount of fruit he had and asked him what they did with it, to which he replied, "We eat what we can, and tin what we can't."' While his listeners were racking their brains trying to find the pun, the speaker was wondering why nobody laughed.

Activity 2 (Groups of 4)

Decide whether the inappropriate use of language that you have identified:

a. is incongruous because it is socio-culturally or grammatically inapplicable.
b. is hilarious because of the use of a word/s other than the one the speaker intended to use.
c. could result in a misunderstanding.
d. results in a breakdown of communication.

Activity 3 (Groups of 4)

Change the language in the dialogues/anecdote, so that it becomes acceptable and appropriate.

Activity 4 (Groups of 4)

Here are some examples of the hilarious effect that the inappropriate use of words can create. They are taken from Richard Sheridan's play *The Rivals* (1775). Identify the inappropriate word and replace it with the right one. Say what the difference in meaning is. (You could consult the dictionary for the meanings.)

a. '... promise to forget this fellow—to illiterate him, I say, quite from your memory.'
b. 'Oh he will dissolve my mystery!'
c. 'I am sorry to say, Sir Anthony, that my affluence over my niece is very small.'
d. 'I thought she had persisted from corresponding with him.'
e. 'His physiognomy is so grammatical!'

Activity 5 (Groups of 4)

Decide what the difference in meaning (if any) is among the sentences in each of the following sets of spoken sentences in terms of one, two or all of the following:

- types of sentences (commands, requests, statements, suggestions, etc.)
- relationshship between participants (formal/informal, formal friendly/informal friendly, etc.)
- attitude of speakers (polite/impolite, certain/uncertain, friendly/hostile, etc.)

a. i. Come and see me tomorrow.
   ii. Could you come and see me tomorrow, please.
   iii. Do come and see me tomorrow.
   iv. Is it possible for you to come and see me tomorrow?
   v. I wonder if you can come and see me tomorrow.

b. i. D'you mind shutting that window?
   ii. Shut that window, will you?
   iii. Shut that window at once.
   iv. Please shut that window.
c. i. Where were you all these days?
   ii. Could you tell me where you were all these days?
   iii. I'd like to know where you were all these days?
   iv. Surely I have the right to know where you were all these days.
   v. Would you like to tell me where you were all these days?
d. i. I'd like to invite you home for lunch tomorrow.
   ii. Come home and have lunch with me tomorrow.
   iii. How about having lunch with me tomorrow?
   iv. I'd love to have you over for lunch tomorrow.
   v. Would you like to have lunch with me tomorrow?

Activity 6 (Groups of 4)

Construct contexts* and write conversations using each of the utterances in at least one set.

Points to ponder (Groups of 4)

Discuss the following questions and give examples in support of your answers. Each group presents their answers to the other groups, and these are discussed.

1. Is the knowledge of grammatical sentences enough to enable appropriate use of these sentences in a given context?
2. Can form and function be treated as entirely separate features, independent of each other in the process of language acquisition?
3. Should teachers focus on fluency or accuracy while teaching speaking? Or should both fluency and accuracy be the goal?
4. What are the techniques that can be used to teach speaking (fluency and/or accuracy)?
5. If you have been teaching speaking, can you tell the other groups what materials you use and what methods/techniques have been successful in your class?
6. Can you think of examples of inappropriate use of language which have any of the effects (a.) to (d.) above?

* the place where the conversation takes place, the participants and their relationship, i.e. formal/informal

Unit 7

Prompting

Students in many schools learn English mainly through reading and writing. Most of their English textbooks comprise passages, stories and poems for reading. These are followed mainly by comprehension, grammar and vocabulary exercises. Sometimes there are passages for listening followed by questions (to test comprehension) which are to be answered in writing. The emphasis on reading and writing almost to the exclusion of listening and speaking deprives students of the opportunity to develop their aural-oral skills which are necessary in the context of the increasing importance of oral communication in the world today. In the absence of sufficient training in the aural-oral skills, students lack the confidence to communicate in English when required to do so.

Given the need for training in speaking, we need to remind ourselves that most students communicate in an Indian language at home and outside the English classroom, which is quite natural. It is in the English class, therefore, that with the help of our materials, we have to strive to develop in them the confidence to express themselves in English. How can we do this?

An effective technique that could motivate learners to speak is prompting. By, prompting, we mean using materials to encourage the student to speak—to break the ice, as it were—starting with one- or two-sentence answers to questions about the prompt, and gradually progressing towards an increase in the quantum of speech from guided to less guided. Eventually, prompting should enable students to express their points of view, with the understanding that on most subjects there can be more than one point of view, and we could have arguments for and against something. Look at an example below of the use of prompts to get students to talk in English.

A picture of two children watching TV with the caption 'Glued to the Television' could be used to ask students what the picture is about and what the word 'glued' means in this context. The students could then work in groups and answer the following questions (orally) which could be written on the blackboard.

a. Do you like watching TV?
b. For how long do you watch TV every day?
c. What programmes do you like best? Why?
d. Do you learn anything from TV programmes?
e. Does watching TV cause you any harm?

Each student in a group should orally answer at least three questions. The representative of each group must note down each member's answers and report them to the other groups. In a higher class (9 or 10), the teacher could take this forward and initiate a discussion based on the statement 'Watching television can cause a great deal of harm.' Students could form groups of those in favour of the statement and those against it. Some points in favour of and against the subject could be provided in order to guide the discussion. For example:

For	Against
a. TV occupies all our leisure hours to the exclusion of other hobbies such as reading books and playing games	a. We can always select the programmes we wish to watch and, therefore, need not spend all our time watching TV.
b. A large number of programmes on TV are of a very poor quality and some are full of violence.	b. But there are programmes that are very informative on channels like 'Discovery Channel', 'Animal Planet' and National Geographic, and we could watch those.

The groups 'for' and 'against' the subject could then discuss the subject and each student in a group could give at least one argument either 'for' or 'against' the statement as the case may be.

Thus, keeping the level of students in mind, one could use the same or similar prompts to encourage/motivate them to speak in English.

Types of prompting

a. Visual prompting

Visual prompting, as input intended to trigger oral communication, can be of different kinds. A picture or a series of pictures in a sequence, a television visual, a photograph, a comic strip, an advertisement for a product and, a painting are all examples of powerful visual prompts.

Note that beginning with a description of what the student sees in the visual provided followed by sharing what they think it is about with the members of their group would help them to start speaking. A story created and told from a picture or a series of pictures can help develop students' understanding of the tenses and enhance their creative ability. A visual prompt can also be used to lead to a discussion of a related subject, for example, the last two prompts in Activity 1 below.

Activity 1 (Groups of 4)

Consider the following as visual prompts and answer the following.

a. Which level/s of students could each one of them be used for? Give reasons.*
b. What would the objective of each prompt be?
c. What activities would you design to achieve the objective/s?
   i. pictures of 5 or 6 types of flowers (in colour), for example rose, jasmine, shoe flower, or hibiscus, sunflower, canna. (objectives: recognising colours, describing, naming, talking about and dislikes, etc.)
   ii. picture of a rainbow (objectives: recognising colours, how they are formed, shape, comparing with other shapes—bent, twisted, wavy, zigzag, etc.)
   iii. a series of pictures that illustrate events in any of the following stories (objectives: describing of each of the pictures using present continuous tense, narrating of stories using present simple/past tense)

The Hare and the Tortoise

A hare one day made fun of the short feet and slow pace of the tortoise, who replied laughing, 'Though you be swift as the wind, I will beat you in a race.' The hare, believing the tortoise's claim to be simply impossible, agreed to the proposal. They agreed that the fox should choose the course and fix the goal. On the day of the race both of them started together. While the tortoise went on at a slow and steady pace to the end of the course, the hare lay down by the wayside and fell asleep. When he woke up and started moving as fast as he could, he saw that the tortoise had already reached the goal and was sleeping because she was tired.

The Monkey and the Fishermen

A monkey perched upon a huge tree saw some fishermen casting their nets into a river, and watched them carefully. The fishermen after a while gave up fishing, and went home for dinner leaving their nets upon the bank. The

* Remember that the same visual prompt could be used for different levels.

monkey, who is better at imitation than most animals, came down from the tree and tried to do as the fishermen had done. He picked up a net and threw it into the river, but became entangled in the mesh and drowned. As he was dying, he said to himself, 'It serves me right, for what business had I who had never handled a net to try and catch fish.'

The Thirsty Crow

One day a crow who was very thirsty went in search of water. He flew around until he reached a garden where he saw a jug with some water in it. But the crow could not reach it because the level was low. The crow was very wise. He thought of a plan to bring up the level of water so that he could drink it. He dropped pebbles into the jug one by one till the water came up. Then he quenched his thirst and flew away.

iv. picture of bees on a comb (objectives: talking about what the picture is about–apiculture, [vocabulary—culture—meaning here: the growing of plants or breeding of particular animals in order to get a particular substance or crop from them, other words with 'culture', e.g. agriculture, horticulture, sericulture]
v. pictures of hatching of snakes (king cobras) and of two men in the act of capturing a cobra (objectives: describing the picture and leading to a discussion on snakes, kinds of snakes, snake parks, snake charmers, mistaken beliefs about snakes, superstitions, snake worship, etc.)
vi. picture of two children watching television with the caption 'Glued to the TV' (objectives: initiate a debate for and against watching TV, its usefulness/advantages, harm/disadvantages in groups [argument/counterargument]
vii. picture of a row of very large felled trees lying by the roadside (debate—environment vs development, expressing opinions—agreeing/disagreeing with the other's point of view)

b. Audio prompting

Another technique that can be used to prompt students to speak is to have them listen to recordings of snippets of news, conversation, announcements, short stories, poems, discussions, etc., and design activities that would enable them to interact with members of their group. In part 1 we have already demonstrated how listening can be effectively linked to speaking. Audio prompting can serve as a base or resource that students draw upon to help them express themselves and participate in a discussion.

Activity 2

Study the following conversations and answer the following.

a. Which level/class would it be most suitable for?

b. What is the objective of each of the conversations?
c. What activities would you design in order to achieve your objective/s?

....

1. A: Have you got a minute?
   B: Err..., mm... Can I see you later?
   A: Will two be a convenient time?
   B: Mm... shall we make it four?
   A: Okay. Thanks. See you at four.
2. A: Hi! What a pleasant surprise! Where were you all these days?
   B: Hi! I was in the village with my grandparents.
   A: No wonder you're looking so relaxed. You seem to have enjoyed yourself.
   B: You bet I have!
3. A: Could you possibly take my suitcase down from the loft?
   B: Certainly. Which one?
   A: That large brown one.
   B: This one?
   A: No, the one on the right.
   B: This one?
   A: Ah, yes. (pause)
   B: Here you are.
   A: Thanks so much.
   B: Pleasure/Not at all.
4. A: Could I see Mr Bhatia?
   B: I'm afraid he's not in.
   A: Could you tell me when he'll be back?
   B: I'm sorry. I don't know.
   A: Would you mind taking a message for him?
   B: Not at all.
5. A: Hello, I'm Raghav. What's your name?
   B: Hello. I'm Madhu. I'm from Kolkata. And you?
   A: I'm from Chennai. (pause) I haven't seen you before.
   B: I've just joined the school.
   A: Which class are you in?
   B: 6 A.
   A: I'm in 6 A too. Come with me. I'll take you there.
   B: Thank you.

6. A: I hope you didn't forget to post my letter.
   B: Oh dear! It slipped my mind. I'm so sorry.
   A: It's urgent. Please do remember to post it today.
   B: I certainly will.
7. A: The annual day is only a month away. What d'you think we should do?
   B: Don't worry. There's plenty of time.
   C: Why don't we meet to plan.
   A: That's a good idea. I suggest we meet this afternoon.
   C: How about sending round a notice right away?
   A: You're right.
8. A: Would you like to see a film?
   B: Which one?
   A: *The Horror of Dracula.*
   B: I don't much care for horror movies.
   A: Shall we go to the circus then?
   B: Oh yes! Thanks. That'd be so much fun.
9. A: Sheila, meet my sister, Radha.
   B: Hello, Radha. Nice to meet you.
   C: Hello, Sheila. Nice to meet you too.
   B: You are taller than your sister.
   A: Yes. And my youngest sister is the tallest of the three of us.
   B: Oh, so the eldest is the shortest and the youngest is the tallest.
   C: Yes, indeed.

Activity 3

Given the following announcements, decide what students ought to know and practise in order to understand them.

a. May I have your attention, please. Train no. 7423 to New Delhi is due to arrive at platform no. three at 20.30 hours.
b. May I have your attention, please. Train no. 2334 leaving for Mumbai at 14.40 hours from platform no. two will now leave at 14.40 hours from platform no. four instead. Passengers waiting on platform two are requested to move to platform four. I repeat—passengers going to Mumbai by train no. 2334 are requested to move to platform four. We are sorry for the inconvenience to passengers.
c. Your attention please. The arrival of train no. 7254 from Kolkata is delayed by one and a half hours. It will now arrive at 09.00 hours instead of 07.30 hours.

or

(Your) Attention please. Train number 7254 from Kolkata, which is scheduled to arrive at 07.30 hours, is one and a half hours late. It will now arrive at 09.00 hours.

d. May I have your attention, please. The principal would like to meet all the class representatives at 2 o'clock this afternoon. Teachers are requested to send them to the principal's office.

e. Classes will be suspended after 1 o'clock this week. Students will have rehearsals in the afternoons to prepare for the annual day. Could the teachers please ensure that students rehearse their parts every afternoon this week.

UNIT 8

FUNCTIONS OF LANGUAGE IN RELATION TO CONTEXT

The language we speak is a vehicle for communicating our ideas and feelings to those sharing that language with us. In other words, communication does not take place in a vacuum. It takes more than one person to interact.

In addition to the participants in a conversation, there are other factors that determine the kind of language we must use. The relationship between participants (formal/informal), the function performed in a particular interaction (meeting and greeting people, enquiring, requesting, apologising, sympathising, describing, narrating, etc.) and the context in which the interaction takes place (social, academic or professional) all have a bearing on the form/structure of oral communication.

In this unit, we shall focus on the use of language for different functions broadly in three contexts—social, academic and professional. Of these contexts, functions for the first two, that is social and academic, would need to be acquired at school whereas those for the professional context could be acquired at college or at different professional institutions.

Use of functions in social contexts

When we consider language functions in social contexts, we refer to socio-culturally appropriate language used to establish and maintain social relationships and are basic to oral communication. Owing to this, the social context sometimes overlaps with academic and professional contexts. Moreover, the language used to perform these functions comprises fixed formulaic expressions which are easy to learn and help the beginner to use socially appropriate language confidently.

Let us read/listen to the following dialogues.

1. A: Excuse me, have you got the time*?
   B: Er, yes. It's a quarter to ten.
   A: Thank you.
   B: You're welcome.
2. A: Hello, B. Nice to see you. How're you?
   B: I'm quite well, thank you. And you?
   A: Oh, I'm fine. Busy as usual.
   B: Haven't seen you for quite some time.
   A: I was out of town for a fortnight, actually.
   B: No wonder. I've been wanting to see you. Could you spare some time for me?
   A: I'm afraid it won't be possible. I'm going to be out of town again for a month.
   B: I see. Maybe we could meet when you return.
   A: Yes. Perhaps.
   B: Thanks all the same. Bye!
   A: Bye!
3. A: Would you like a drink?
   B: Yes, please.
   A: What would you like?
   B: Fresh lime and soda, please.
   A: Certainly. I'll be back with it in a minute.
   B: Thank you very much.
   A: (My) pleasure.
4. A: Excuse me, could you tell me the way to the public library, please.
   B: How should I know. I don't belong here.
   A: I'm sorry.
   B: Oh, that's all right.
5. A: I say, I'm so sorry about this. I didn't intend to miss your show.
   B: I was so disappointed to see you weren't there. But I suppose it can't be helped.
   A: My brother suddenly took ill, so we rushed him to hospital.
   B: That's unfortunate. How's he now?
   A: Better, thanks.

* This is used in British English as an alternative to 'What time is it?'

6. A: I would like to apologise for not attending the meeting.
   B: It's a pity you missed it. We took some important decisions.
   A: I wonder if it would be possible to know what decisions were taken.
   B: Well, you could talk to Chandra. She'll tell you all about it, I'm sure.
   A: Thank you.
7. A: Please ensure that no child leaves the campus alone.
   B: Certainly, sir. We'll do our best.
   A: If any child is not picked up by a parent/guardian, they must be contacted immediately.
   B: Yes, sir.
8. A: Where on earth were you? I've been looking around for you desperately.
   B: Went out of town. Why? What's up?
   A: In spite of our protest, they've cut down twelve more trees!
   B: This is an emergency. We must meet this afternoon and decide what to do.
   A: Yes, that's why I was looking for you.
9. A: Hello, Bhavana. What can I do for you?
   B: Could you attest my certificates, please.
   A: Certainly. What for?
   B: I'm going to apply for a job.
   A: Here you are. Best of luck!
   B: Thank you so much. Bye, bye!
   A: Bye! Let me know how you fare.
   B: I will.
10. A: I heard your mother's no more.
    B: She passed away two days ago.
    A: I'm so sorry. She was such a dear.
    B: We're all going to miss her terribly.
    A: I can't believe she's no more. I spoke to her only last week.
11. A: Good morning! I'm Anandi from Mysore.
    B: Pleased to meet you, Anandi. I'm Bhavesh from Kolkata.
    A: Glad to meet you. Has your son won an award?
    B: Yes. Yours too?
    A: No. My grandson's won an award.
    B: How lovely! Congratulations!
    A: Thank you. Congratulations to you too.
    B: Thank you.
12. A: Where were you yesterday? You missed two important classes—maths and physics.
    B: I went to the Commonwealth games. It was such fun.

A: But it's against the rules.

B: Nobody found out. So it's okay.

A: No, it isn't. I don't think you should stay away without permission.

B: What should I do now?

A: If I were you, I'd apply for leave right away.

B: All right. I suppose I'd better do that.

Activity 1 (Groups of 4)

Read/listen to each of the above dialogues and answer the following. Some options are given to you in brackets.

a. What is the relationship between the participants? (formal/informal, friendly, intimate)
b. Where do you think the conversation takes place? (at home, in an office, at a bus station, at school/college, at a railway station, etc.)
c. What function do the participants perform? (greeting, enquiring, requesting, etc.)*
d. What language/expressions do the participants use to perform the functions?
e. Are the expressions used appropriate to the social context you have constructed?

Activity 2 (Groups of 4)

Share your observations with the other groups.

Activity 3 (Groups of 4)

Look at the function(s) the participants perform in the dialogues above and list as many alternative expressions/structures as you know, which are used to perform the same function(s). Representatives of each group can write them on the blackboard.

Activity 4 (Groups of 4)

Think of three other functions related to social contexts and list the language expressions that are used to perform them.

* Note that they could be performing more that one function in some cases.

Use of functions in academic contexts

Functions in academic contexts are closely related to the subject being taught/learnt. In other words, the topic of a conversation or a discussion determines the language used to perform a particular function.

ACTIVITY 5 (GROUPS OF 4)

Look at the following piece from an English reader for class 2 English-medium students in Andhra Pradesh. Decide what specific sub-skill in speaking it would help the student to acquire.

> Look at this map of India. There are mighty Himalayas in the north. These mountains are very high. They rise to the sky. There is snow on the top of these mountains. The mountains look beautiful. There are seas on three sides of our country. There is the Bay of Bengal on the east, the Indian Ocean on the south and the Arabian Sea on the west. In summer, the snow on the Himalayas melts into water. The big rivers of the north spring from the Himalayas. The Indus, the Ganges and the Brahmaputra are the three big rivers of the north. They flow down the hills, through the valleys across the plains into the sea. There are large plains in the north of India. People grow wheat and maize there.
>
> In the south, there are three big rivers, the Godavari, the Krishna and the Cauvery. There are large dams across these rivers. The Nagarjunasagar Dam is across the river Krishna in Andhra Pradesh. People grow rice, maize and ragi in the south.

ACTIVITY 6 (GROUPS OF 4)

Pick out sentences that would be relevant to the specific subskill in speaking for students of classes 2 and 3.

ACTIVITY 7 (GROUPS OF 4)

With reference to the sentences that you have picked out, discuss what aspects of language (vocabulary, grammar, pronunciation) you would concentrate on in order to teach students at this level the particular subskill in speaking. Share your ideas with other groups.

ACTIVITY 8

What activities (including follow-up activities) would you devise in order to help students acquire the subskill.

Activity 9 (Groups of 4)

Decide whether this passage could be used for developing the same subskill in higher classes (classes 4 and 5). If you decide that it could be used, then would you add more sentences (from the text) to those you have already picked out?

Activity 10

Decide what aspects of language (vocabulary, grammar, pronunciation) students at this level would need to learn in order to develop this subskill in speaking.

Activity 11

Design at least three activities in addition to the basic ones you have already designed to enable students of class 4/5 to use this subskill effectively.

Activity 12 (Groups of 4)

Look at the following excerpt from an essay entitled 'The Sporting Spirit' by George Orwell, included in the English reader for class 9, Karnataka (pp. 133–137) and decide what activities you would design to enable students to understand the two points of view the author presents regarding sport—other peoples' and his own.

> I am always amazed when I hear people saying that sport creates goodwill between nations, and that if only the common peoples of the world could meet one another at football or cricket, they would have no inclinations to meet on the battlefield. Even if one didn't know from concrete examples (the 1936 Olympic Games, for instance) that international sporting contests lead to revelries of hatred, one could deduce it from general principles.
>
> Nearly all the sports practiced nowadays are competitive. You play to win, and the game has little meaning unless you do your utmost to win. On the village green, where you pick up sides and no feeling of local patriotism is involved, it is possible to play simply for the fun and exercise but as soon as the question of prestige arises, as soon as you feel that you and some larger unit will be disgraced if you lose, the most savage combative instincts are aroused. Anyone who has played even in a school football match knows this. At the international level sport is frankly mimic warfare. But the significant thing is not the behaviour of the players but the attitude of the spectators: and behind the spectators of the nations who work themselves into furies over these absurd contests, and seriously believe—at any rate for short periods—that running, jumping, and kicking a ball are tests of national virtue.

ACTIVITY 13 (GROUPS OF 4)

In the context provided, what functions of language would your students need to acquire?

ACTIVITY 14 (GROUPS OF 4)

Design activities to help students to express their own point of view regarding sport and substantiate it with examples*.

ACTIVITY 15

Representatives of each group will present the results of activities 12, 13 and 14 you have prepared (in 1 and 3) to the other groups and list them on the blackboard.

ACTIVITY 16

As follow-up to the earlier set of activities, construct other contexts in which there could be more than one point of view. Design activities to help students present their own point of view regarding the context/s provided.

ACTIVITY 17

Look at another extract which has been adapted from the English reader for class 8, Tamil Nadu (pp. 78–79). It is a dialogue between a student who is selected to represent Tamil Nadu at the National Level Hockey Tournament at Bhubaneshwar and her school physical education teacher. Pick out the expressions that are used to perform some specific functions in the context.

Vaishnavi: Excuse me, ma'am. May I come in?

PET: Come in.

Vaishnavi: Good morning, ma'am.

PET: Good morning, Vaishnavi. How's your preparation for the tournament (going)?

Vaishnavi: It's slowed down a bit.

PET: Why? What's the matter? You seem to be worried.

Vaishnavi: Ma'am, my mother thinks it's a waste of time. She says I mustn't miss classes. If I do, my studies will suffer. What should I do?

* Encourage the use of alternative phrases to perform the function.

PET: I don't think you should give this up. It's a rare opportunity.

Vaishnavi: Indeed it is. But my mother thinks my studies are more important.

PET: I'd advise you to see the principal about this.

Vaishnavi: D'you think the principal will solve the problem?

PET: Most certainly. I think you ought to make a request for special classes to make up for what you'll miss.

Vaishnavi: That's a good idea. I'll do it, straightaway. Thank you so much, ma'am.

PET: Not at all.

ACTIVITY 18

Suggest some activities you would design in order to reinforce these functions.

ACTIVITY 19

What other contexts and activities would you construct in order to ensure that these functions are performed appropriately?

ACTIVITY 20

Can you think of alternative expressions to perform these functions? Do you consider it worthwhile to make students aware of them? If so, what activities would you prepare to help them use these expressions as well?

ACTIVITY 21

Construct contexts to demonstrate the use of at least two of the following functions. Underline the phrases/expressions used to perform them.

a. Making suggestions
b. Making comparisons
c. Agreeing and disagreeing with opinions
d. Talking about past events
e. Expressing likes and dislikes
f. Making a complaint and responding to one

Activity 22

Which of the functions we have mentioned in activity 21 would you teach students of classes 8, 9 and 10? Which ones would you omit? Give reasons.

Activity 23

The following set of sentences is adapted from the class 5 (second language) English reader, Karnataka (p.13).

Look at these clocks.
They are wall clocks.
They are round.
They have two hands—the small hand and the long hand.
The small hand is the hour hand.
It takes one hour to move from one number to the next.
The long hand is the minute hand.
It takes five minutes to move from one number to the next.

The numbers on the clock stand for hours and minutes. The number 12 is at the top and then there are numbers 1 to 11 right round the clock from right to left. Between any two numbers there are five lines that stand for the minutes. After five minutes the long hand moves to the next number. Each of the lines stands for one minute or sixty seconds. So sixty seconds make a minute and sixty minutes make one hour. When the minute hand goes round from 12 to 12 once, the hour hand moves to the next number. Look at these clocks and tell the time.

When both the hands are on 12 it is twelve o'clock.
Look at this clock.

When the long hand is on six and the short hand is between any two numbers, it is half past the hour. For example, look at the following clocks.

When the long hand is on three and the short hand is on some number it is quarter *past* the hour, or fifteen minutes past the hour. Similarly, when the long hand is on nine and the short hand is on some number, it is a quarter *to* the hour.

Decide whether this lesson would help your students to tell the time in English. If yes, decide what techniques you would adopt to help your students understand the concept of time—to count the minutes and the hours.

Activity 24

Prepare activities to demonstrate the order you would follow to teach the alternative expressions used to tell the time (the hour, a quarter past the hour, half past the hour, etc.).

PART 1

APPENDIX 1: NOTES FOR THE TEACHER

It is common knowledge that a child begins to learn a language by listening to it constantly in context. In fact, children learn to speak only after they have had a tremendous amount of input through listening. In a second language learning situation, however, it is rare for the learner to be exposed to the second language in a natural environment. Most second language learning takes place in a simulated context, where most listening also takes place. We as teachers have to work to create contexts that would be as close to a natural environment as possible. In order to do this, we need to make a note of the kinds of situations in which our students are likely to listen to spoken English.

Why do our students need to listen to spoken English? What benefits would they derive from listening? Training in listening will help them improve their English. They will learn new words and their relatedness in a particular context. Contextualised grammatical structures as used by speakers would ensure the correct use of those structures. Moreover, it would prepare students to listen to talks and lectures in their academic/professional courses. Besides, being a good listener is an added advantage in group discussions and debates.

Listening comprehension has by and large been tested in most English language courses probably on the assumption that it was taught at some stage in the language learning process. But recent school textbooks in English belie this assumption. Exercises in listening test rather than teach it. The student is asked to listen to a particular story/ passage and answer questions or, sometimes, fill in the blanks.

What is the difference between teaching and testing listening? Testing a skill is the end-product of the process of learning that skill. Thus, when we test listening, we assume that the learner has already learnt what to listen for and how to listen, and approach it as an integrated whole. However, in order to achieve the latter we need to go through the process of familiarising ourselves with the parts that make up the whole. In other words, since we listen with a purpose, the learners must be prepared for what they are going to listen to. One can listen for the general message of a particular piece or for factual information which one needs to make a note of, or listen for detail and then draw inference from what has been said. One could also use listening as a take-off point for a discussion.

Let us consider the following listening passage taken from a Karnataka State Board English reader for class 4. It is about the dog and the bone—one of Aesop's fables.

> A dog was carrying a large bone in his mouth and was feeling pleased with himself. He walked across the fields and through the woods until he came to a bridge across a stream. As he was walking across he looked down and saw another dog, just like him, with a bone just like his. It was his own reflection, but the dog did not realise this. As the dog looked, he felt more and more unhappy. 'That dog has a bone like mine, only his is much bigger,' he said. The dog became very jealous. He decided that his own bone was not good enough and that he would drop it so that he could take the other dog's bone. Splash! He dropped his bone into the water, and then he saw what a fool he had been. There was no other bone. His meal was now at the bottom of the stream. The dog went home with nothing.

The students listen to the story with their books closed and again with their books open. The text is followed by the following questions.

What did the dog have in his mouth?
What did the dog find when he looked into the stream?
Why did the dog feel unhappy?
When did the dog realise he was a fool?
Why was the dog left with nothing?

These questions test the student's listening comprehension straightaway. However, if we were to put up some words from the passage with their meanings on the blackboard before we read the story, it would help the student to listen for those words in the story and understand their relationship to other words. For example, the following words could be listed on the board to help the students prepare to listen to the story.

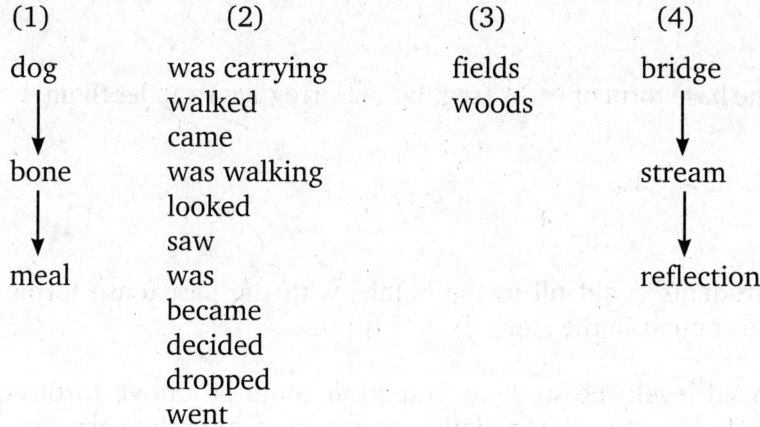

Activity 1

Working in groups, let students listen to the story, paying attention to the words in the first column on the blackboard. Ask each group to tell the others what the story is about in one sentence and to also give the story a title. (Encourage students to be original and come up with different titles.) Put the titles up on the blackboard.

Activity 2

Let the students listen to the story for what the dog did. While they listen, let them look at the words in the second column on the blackboard and the questions in the textbook. These are intended to act as prompts to enable the student follow the sequence of events.

Activity 3

Link the past tense forms of regular and irregular verbs to their use in storytelling. For example:

regular verb	*past tense*	*irregular verb*	*past tense*
walk	walked	come	came
look	looked	see	saw
carry	carried	is	was
drop	dropped	go	went
decide	decided	become	became
		do	did

Activity 4

Give students a list of the base form of verbs (regular and irregular) and let them write their past tense forms.

Activity 5

Given the infinitives, students could fill in the blanks with the past tense forms of verbs appropriate to the context in the story.

Note: At a more advanced level, the students' attention could be drawn to the use of the base form of the verb with 'do' in negative sentences, where the past tense is indicated by 'did not' and not the past tense form of the main verb.

For example: '… the dog did not *realise* this.'

Activity 6 (Groups of 6)

Ask students what lesson they have learnt from the story. Let each group tell the rest of the class what lesson the story has taught them.

——→ lesson ——→ fable

Activity 7

Follow up activity 6 by linking listening to speaking. Let the students narrate the story they have listened to. This activity can be used to stress on the correct use of past tense forms of verbs for storytelling.

Activity 8

Move on to a less guided activity by asking students to narrate a story they have read or listened to.

These activities will help in guiding the students in listening. Students will be able to take a test in listening as a whole only after they have learnt to listen for the parts that comprise that whole. In other words, we need to take them through the process before arriving at the end product.

Listening Materials

As we have already said, the second language learner can pick up a considerable amount of the language (here, English) from the contexts to which they are exposed. For example, they probably listen to radio and television programmes in English, to announcements at railway/bus stations, airports, etc., to their English teacher in the class, their subject teachers (in English-medium schools) and their peers. We need to, as far as possible, replicate these contexts in order to train students to listen for the message as a whole and, at the same time, be able to select the information they require.

In addition to listening for information, detail, etc., students also acquire the language used in different contexts for different subjects. For example, the past tense forms of words is generally used to tell a story, and the base form of the verb is generally used to describe an experiment, a process, a game, a person, etc. The student is also exposed to useful nouns and adjectives relating to the kind of listening input.

Listening, therefore, is essentially a broad-based activity and extends beyond the facts that are conveyed in the materials. It is intended to draw the listener's attention to the vocabulary, grammar and usage relating to the context in the listening input, then extend the use of these to other similar contexts in real life to ensure that they have been understood and learnt. This can be done through speaking activities, information transfer and writing activities. Listening materials, therefore, can act as a springboard for developing other skills as well.

In the initial stages (classes 1, 2 and 3), listening materials should help the learner get accustomed to the sounds of English, to similar sounding words—rhyming words—and their meaning, the base forms of simple verbs, (for example 'go', 'eat', 'play', 'work') etc. Encouraging students to write the words on the blackboard can help them associate the written word (its spelling) with what it sounds like—its pronunciation. Nursery rhymes, songs would serve as effective listening input. The teacher's instructions in class can be useful for helping students understand them and carry them out.

At the primary (classes 4 and 5), middle (classes 6, 7 and 8) and high school (classes 9 and 10) levels, dialogues that are as close to real-life situations as possible can be used to sensitise students to the difference between the written word (spelling) and the spoken word (sound), to word stress, sentence stress, and rhythm and tone. The activities should be so designed as to suit the level of the class being trained.

Ideally, listening materials should be drawn from live radio and television broadcasts, conversations/dialogues, announcements at railway/bus stations, airports, sports events, and entertainment programmes. Since recording live events is not always possible, dialogues and materials from the students' English textbooks can be selected for teaching listening. Materials can also be designed based on the students' social science textbooks as they comprise subjects that are of current and general interest, for example the environment and its preservation, civic duties, responsibilities and civil rights, and important personalities and their contributions to the society.

The advantage in using students' textbooks to prepare listening materials is that it helps them understand the content and the language better so then they are less likely to attempt the exercises that follow the text mechanically. Listening to a story, for example, enables a child to remember the events and the language and use these to retell the story. The activity will not be entirely new or unfamiliar to either students or teachers as listening to/and telling stories is very much a part of the ancient Indian oral tradition.

Activity types

The type of activity we select would depend largely upon the nature of the materials chosen and the aim of a particular listening exercise. In general, the following activity types could provide a bank from which you can draw depending upon the level of your students in terms of their proficiency in English and the extent of training they have had in listening. The following are some of the activity types you could draw upon. Essentially, most listening activities should be followed by 'doing' ,that is, recognising the content (subject and matter) and form (grammar and vocabulary) and using these in other similar contexts (speaking and writing).

1. The dictionary can be used to find out the meanings of words related to the subject matter of the listening materials. These words can be used in the context that is provided by filling in the blanks. This can be followed up by using the words in a context similar to the one given.
2. Some of the words and phrases can be used as clues that lead the students to the meaning and message of what they listen to.
3. Information transfer, for example filling in maps, charts, tables, marking routes (by following directions, instructions) and filling in diagrams from description, can be linked to speaking by making the students reconstruct the information and convey it to the group/class.
4. Students can be asked to carry out instructions (simple to complex depending on the level of the students). For example, you can give instructions like the following:
   Please open the windows.
   Listen to the poem as it is read out. Then repeat each line after the teacher.
   Listen for the words in the poem that sound similar.
   Add other words that sound like the words in the list.
   Write at least two words that sound like each of the given words.
   Describe a process or an experiment (audio with video support ——> only audio (given about ten words).
   These exercises can be linked to speaking by asking each student/group to give instructions to the class on how to make something of their choice.

5. Students can be made to recognise verb forms (tenses), nouns, adjectives relating to a particular genre (poetry, drama), description of a particular process, instructions, directions, discussion of a particular subject, reporting, etc., in a given context.
6. The above exercise can be linked to speaking by extending the use of these to other similar contexts like storytelling, reporting an incident, reporting an experiment, demonstrating a process (for example, method to make a drink, cook a dish or make a kite, discussing an issue arising from the listening material (that is, expressing opinions, agreeing or disagreeing with a point of view and making suggestions for improvement in the existing state of affairs).
7. Dictation (first at slow speed, then at normal speed) is a useful exercise as it helps students relate the pronunciation of words to their written forms. It also helps students in the higher classes develop an ear for the rhythm of the language.

Sample Materials

The sample materials for listening in Appendix 5 are only illustrations of what could comprise listening materials, and the types of activities teachers could use to enable students to become good listeners and proficient users of English as a second/third language. Though the activities that follow listening texts are by and large intended to be progressively advanced, the order in which they are given need not be rigidly followed. If the teacher feels some of the earlier activities are too easy for their students, they could select those activities that would be suitable and interesting for them. On the other hand, if the teacher feels that doing the simpler/easier exercises successfully would give their students a sense of achievement and encourage them to attempt the more difficult ones, then they could proceed accordingly. More importantly, they could design other activities/exercises to supplement the ones already given. In addition to the texts used as samples, teachers could select their own listening texts and design activities that flow from them. The pronunciation of words could form an integral part of the activities relating to a particular text. But a listening text need not necessarily be selected exclusively for the purpose of designing pronunciation exercises.

The level(s) of students for whom a particular listening text would be suitable is indicated against each sample. However, these are only approximate and are guided by the textbooks of English and social science/environmental studies prescribed by boards of school education in all the four southern states. We believe it would be presumptuous to fix the exact level of the student for whom a particular listening text would be suitable across an entire region. This decision is left to the discretion of the teacher.

The activities have by and large been designed for groups with a view to encouraging participation and helping the weaker students gain confidence. Sometimes, examples (of how an exercise is to be done) have been given in order to ensure that students understand what is expected of them.

Though the sample materials comprise listening input for four different purposes, they need not be treated as discrete units. The division into separate sections is intended to:

a. expose the student to the different kinds of input they are likely to receive in their daily lives.
b. create an awareness in the student of the possible purposes for which they may need to listen, depending on the input. For example, announcements, weather reports and news headlines would provide listening input mainly for information; narratives, passages on matters of general/current interest, discussions, etc. would provide them with input that requires attention to detail, makes them draw inferences and provides an effective link to speaking—for example, by expressing opinions, agreeing or disagreeing with a point of view and giving suggestions.

In addition to the content of listening input, the form, that is, the vocabulary, grammar and usage in a particular context, is also focused on in the activities with a view to enabling students to use English appropriately.

PART 1

APPENDIX 2: ANSWER KEY

Unit 2

ACTIVITY 4

Word/Phrase	*Meaning*
inconsolable	very sad and not possible to comfort
juvenile	connected with young people who are not yet adults
culpable homicide	responsible/to be blamed for killing somebody deliberately
frustration	annoyance and impatience at not being able to do what one wants to
convicted	decided officially in court that somebody is guilty of a crime
ramming into	hitting or running into another vehicle
let off	not to punish somebody for something wrong they have done or to give them only a light punishment
crack down	severe action to restrict the activities of those who go against the law
at the wheel	in the driver's seat of a vehicle
charged with	accused formally of a crime
get away with	to do something wrong and be punished lightly for it

Activity 14

d. i. They would learn to follow the teacher's instructions.
   ii. They would learn to appreciate rhyme.
   iii. They would be exposed to new words.
   iv. They would learn the correct pronunciation of words.
   v. They would learn about doing words, or verbs of action.

Unit 3

Activity 1

January February March April May June

1000 950 900 850 800 750 700 650 600 550 500 450 400 350 300 250 200 150 100 50 10

Events

Junta

ACTIVITY 6

S No.	*Tour package*	*Places*	*Duration of tour*	*Stay*	*Charges to and from starting pt.*	*Other expenses*
1.	Himachal tour package	Kalka, Shimla, Manali, Kullu	5 nights, 6 days	accommodation with breakfast	₹ 25,999 for two	taxes, travel to kalka, lunch and dinner
2.	Kashmir tour package	Srinagar, Gulmarg, Pahalgam	6 nights, 7 days	accommodation in 2/3-star hotels with breakfast and houseboat with all meals	₹ 29,999 for two, car for sightseeing tours from and to Srinagar	travel to Srinagar, lunch and dinner when not on houseboat
3.	Kerala back-water tour package	Kochi, Munnar, Alleppey	3 nights, 4 days	3-star hotels with breakfast and houseboat with all meals	₹ 16,000 for two	travel by road/rail to Kochi, lunch and dinner
4.	Corbett wildlife tour	Corbett National Park	2 nights, 3 days	accommodation with breakfast	₹ 6000 for two includes pick up and drop out railway station	travel to Ramnagar, lunch and dinner

Unit 4

ACTIVITY 2

Panelist's name	*Profession/occupation/designation*	*Area of specialisation*
a. Purvi Chutani	lawyer	cross border immigration issues and adoption issues
b. Shobha Jagtiani	lawyer	issues related to inheritance, succession and taxation

c. Ram Jethmalani	lawyer in the Supreme Court, activist	issues related to domestic violence and abuse
d. Kahim Merchant	painter, executive director of Merchant	Media
e. Satya Sagar	editor of a women's magazine *Need* from DNA	

Activity 3

Question: Shobha, ... what it is we need to know about what we are entitled to as women when there's a will or no will?

Shobha: Indian constitution ⟶ freedom of religion

freedom to be govnd. by pers. law. So depends whether Hindu, Muslim, Xian, Parsi, Jew, etc.

Hindu family ⟶ Hindu Succn Act ⟶ daughter's share = son's

But 'equal share' applies in ind. prop. of father.

Up to 2005 all India law ⟶ daughter no share in Hindu undivided fam. prop.

But some states—progr. step.

1994 Maharashtra amendmt daughter's share = son even in Hindu und^{vd} prop.

Muslims—Shariat Act—daughter's share = ½ that of brother.

Even a will can't remedy this much. Muslim law ⟶ only 1/3 prop. can be beq^{d}.

But Hindu law ⟶ entire prop. can be beq^{d}. by will, i.e. father can disinherit daughter by making a will.

Note: The conventional abbreviations used here are:

=	equal to	⅓	one-third
i.e.	that is	½	half
etc.	etcetera		

Other abbreviations that have been invented are:

govnd:	governed	prop.:	property
pers.:	personal	beq^{d}:	bequeathed
Xian:	Christian	und^{vd}:	undivided
=:	equal to	progr.:	progressive
amend^{t}:	amendment		

Activity 5

To reconstruct these notes you need to use complete grammatical sentences and use the full forms of words in place of their abbreviated forms.

Activity 7

a. Yes.
b. No. They have to be adopted under two different acts—the Hindu Act and the Guardian and Wards Act.
c. No. Only the one adopted under the Hindu Act has full inheritance rights.
d. We need to make a will to protect the second child's rights.

Activity 8

Your discussion need not necessarily be based on real-life examples. You could think of hypothetical/possible reasons for the will to be challenged.

Activity 10

a. 'Maintenance and support' refers to the money a wife gets from her husband when they are separated/divorced.
b. No.
c. The panellist would like to draw the attention of the listener to those situations in our day-to-day life in which women are denied the right to be treated as individuals. She probably feels that there need to be provisions other than those under the law that can ensure that a woman has full rights.
d. No.
e. The anchor confines the discussion of women's rights to the letter of the law.
f. Rani refers to the broad provision under the constitution of the right to equality and equality before the law. So one will ultimately go to the highest law to agitate for something. She also says that once the constitutional provision of equality is enacted it would be a contradiction of the law to say that a widow has a limited position or that a woman does not have the right to be a coheir to ancestral property.

Activity 12

There are hesitation phenomena such as 'er…'. There is repetition or rephrasing of what the speaker wishes to say, for example Shobha says '… under the Muslim law only… er... two-third of the property… er… one-third of the property can be bequeathed.' Shobha rephrases her sentence because she realises she has used the word 'only' which refers to the small proportion of property that can be bequeathed under Muslim law.

Phrases like 'you know' are sometimes used in speech. For example:

a. When the anchor asks what happens when a will is contested, the panellist says, 'Suppose er,... *you know*, a... and the son says *you know*...'
b. A panellist says, 'No I would actually go deeper ..., that is, if there is a certain amount of er,... *you know*, you are not given ... in fact.'

Given these features in the discussion the panellists are participating in, we ask ourselves why these features recur in their speech. This is so because the panellists are thinking at the same time as they speak. In order to give themselves some time to put their thoughts into words, they use 'conversation fillers', such as 'you know'. (Other fillers generally used in conversation include, for example, 'you see', 'I mean'.) Sometimes while they are thinking of the right word or expression to express their thoughts, speakers pause and use 'er' or 'hmm'. At other times they make a false start, and then feel the need to rephrase what they began saying. These are features that characterise spoken language and distinguish it from written language. When we write, we are aware that we are addressing an audience that is not present and that may vary from time to time. Therefore we must make our message succinct. We are able to achieve this because we have a good deal of time to think when we write. As a result the written word, which is recorded is relatively more permanent. The spoken word, on the other hand, is more tentative because it is generally relevant to a specific context.

Note that when we listen to discussions, debates, interviews, etc., we must take care not to allow our attention to be diverted from the main argument by the features mentioned above. These need to be accepted and recognised as part and parcel of spoken English.

Unit 5

Activity 2

As examples, dialogues 1 and 2 are taken up here.

Dialogue 1: Vowels

The letter 'o' is:

— pronounced as in 'cot' in cross, confident.

— pronounced as in 'go' in 'flowing', 'joking', 'over', 'don't' and 'so'

— pronounced as in 'hut' in 'above'

The letter 'e' is:

— pronounced as in 'get' in 'let's'

— pronounced as in 'bit' in be

— generally not pronounced or in slow speech, is pronounced as in 'father' in 'dangerous'

— pronounced as in 'father' in 'problem', 'over' and 'river'

— pronounced (like the 'ee' in 'feet') and (the second 'e') is silent as in 'immediately'

The letter 'a' is:

— pronounced like the letter 'e' in 'father' in 'as'

— pronounced as in 'rate' in 'danger'

— pronounced like the 'e' in 'mother' as in 'above'

— pronounced as in 'fast' in 'mark'

— pronounced like the letters 'au' in 'caught' in 'all'

The letter 'i' is:

— pronounced as in 'right' in 'quite' and 'might'

Dialogue 1: Consonants

The letter 'c' (and the letters 'ck') is:

— pronounced as in 'cat' in 'cross', 'quickly', 'can' and 'confident'

The letter 's' (or the letters 'ss') is:

— pronounced as in 'sea' in 'cross'

— pronounced as in 'zoo' in 'as' and 'river's' (the shortened form of 'is')

The letter 'r' is not pronounced in British English when:

— it occurs finally in an isolated word as in 'river'

— it occurs before consonants as in 'mark'

The letter 'd' is silent in 'bridge'.

The letter 'g' is pronounced like the 'j' in 'joke'.

The letters 'll' in 'all' and 'well' represent only one sound as in 'luck'.

The letter 'l' is silent in 'should'.

The letters 'ou' in 'should' are pronounced as in 'put'.

The letters 'gh' are silent in 'right'.

Dialogue 2: Vowels

The letters 'ou' in 'you' are pronounced like the 'oe' in 'shoes'

The letter 'u' in 'just' is pronounced like the 'u' in 'cup'.

The letter 'ou' in 'about' is pronounced like the 'ow' in 'cow'.

The letters 'ou' in 'your' is pronounced like the 'aw' in 'saw' or the 'ure' in 'pure'.

The letters 'oo' in 'look' is pronounced like the 'u' in 'put'.

The letters 'oo' in 'too' is pronounced like the 'u' in 'flute'.

The letters 'oo' in 'door' is pronounced like the 'au' in 'taught'.

The letters 'oo' in 'good' is pronounced like the 'u' in 'put'.
The letter 'a' in 'rather' is pronounced like the 'a' in 'last'.
The letter 'a' in 'am' is pronounced like the 'a' in 'cat'.
The letter 'a' in 'can't' is pronounced like the 'a' in 'fast'.
The letter 'a' in 'what' is pronounced like the 'o' in 'not'.
The letter 'a' in 'many' is pronounced like the 'e' in 'get'.
The letter 'a' in 'matter' is pronounced like the 'a' in 'bat'.

Dialogue 2: Consonants

The letters 't' in 'get' and 'tt' in 'matter' represent the same sound.
The letter 'n' in 'can't', 'many' and the letters 'gn' in 'sign' represent the same sound.
The letter 's' in 'upset', 'just', 'what's', 'disturb' and 'sign' represents the sound of 's' in 'sea'.
but
The letter 's' in 'interruptions' is pronounced like the 'z' in 'zoo'.
The letters 'rr' in 'interruptions' is pronounced like the 'r' in 'rose'.

Activity 3

You must have noticed that there are the following types of mismatch between spelling and sound in English.

a. The same vowel letter/s represent/s different sounds. (For example 'a' in 'rather', 'can't', 'what', 'many' and 'matter' in dialogue 2 represents different sounds. The same consonant letter/s represent/s different consonant sounds. (For example, 's' in 'must' and 'as' in dialogue 1 represents different consonant sounds.)
b. Different vowel and consonant letters represent the same sound. (For example, in dialogue 2 the vowel letters 'ou' in 'you', 'oo' in 'too' and 'o' in 'do' represent the same vowel sound as 'ue' in 'blue' and the letter 'y' in 'why' and 'i' in 'light' represent the same sound. Similarly, 'ss' in 'cross' and 's' in 'dangerous' represent the same sound, and 'rr', 'r' in 'interruptions' and 'right' respectively, and 'g' in 'dangerous' and 'dg' in 'bridge' represent the same consonant sound.
c. There are letters that are silent in the pronunciation of a word. (For example, 'd' and 'e' in 'bridge' and 'g' in 'sign', 'joking' and 'putting'.
d. Some letters represent two consonant sounds, for example, 'q' in 'quickly' and 'quite' represents a combination of two sounds—'k' as in 'kite' and 'w' as in 'watch'. Similarly, you will notice that the letter 'x' also represents two sounds—'k' as in 'kite' and 's' as in 'sea'. The words 'expect' and 'expert' in dialogue 5 are examples. You could add to these examples as you listen to dialogue 3 onwards.

ACTIVITIES 4 AND 5

Refer to the materials in Appendix 3 and listen to a recording of these on the CD.

ACTIVITIES 8 AND 11

DIALOGUE 1

A: Let's ˈcross the ˈbridge as quickly as we can.

B: You must be ˈjoking. It's quite dangerous to cross it. The river's ˈflowing above the ˈdanger ˈmark.

A: I ˈdon't ˈthink so. It ˈshouldn't be a ˈproblem if we ˈcross over imˈmediately.

B: ˈAll ˈright. Since you're so ˈconfident we ˈmight as well.

DIALOGUE 2

A: You look ˈrather upˈset

B: I ˈam upset. I just ˈcan't get ˈon with my ˈwork.

A: ˈWhy? ˈWhat's the ˈmatter?

B: There are ˈtoo ˈmany interˈruptions.

A: ˈWhat about ˈputting up a 'Doˈnot-diˈsturb' ˈsign on your ˈdoor?

B: ˈGood iˈdea.

DIALOGUE 3

A: I've ˈgot to deˈcide by this ˈevening.

B: ˈSorry? I ˈdidn't ˈget what you ˈsaid. Deˈcide ˈwhat?

A: ˈWhere I should ˈtake the ˈchildren on ˈSunday.

B: ˈDidn't you ˈsay you were ˈgoing to the ˈzoo?

A: ˈYes. But ˈmany of the ˈchildren would preˈfer to ˈgo to the ˈcircus.

B: Then we'll diˈvide them into ˈtwo ˈgroups. ˈYou can ˈgo with ˈone ˈgroup and ˈI'll go with the ˈother.

A: ˈYes. ˈThanks a ˈlot.

DIALOGUE 4

A: We'll ˈhave to ˈhurry if we ˈwant to ˈcatch the 8 aˈ.m. to the uniˈversity.

B: ˈDon't ˈworry. There's ˈplenty of ˈtime.

A: But we've ˈgot to ˈwait for the ˈothers.

B: We ˈdon't ˈhave to. We can ˈleave a ˈmessage. ˈTell them we're on our ˈway.

A: Oh, ˈthere they ˈare. ˈNow we can ˈall ˈleave toˈgether.

Dialogue 5

A: ˈHow did you ˈlike it?

B: ˈFascinating! It's ˈalways a ˈpleasure to ˈlisten to him.

A: He ˈmakes it all ˈsound so ˈsimple.

B: ˈJust what we'd exˈpect of an ˈexpert.

A: He's an exˈceptionally ˈgood ˈspeaker. ˈIsn't he?

B: (There's) ˈNo ˈdoubt about it.

Dialogue 6

A: Well, it's been so ˈnice ˈtalking to you.

B: ˈThanks for ˈmaking ˈtime to ˈsee me.

A: (My) ˈPleasure. I ˈwonder what the ˈtime is?

B: Er.., It's ˈnearly ˈtwelve.

A: ˈTwelve! Alˈready! I must ˈhurry, or I'll ˈmiss my ˈflight. Bye, ˈbye.

B: ˈBye, and ˈthanks aˈgain.

Dialogue 7

A: I just ˈcan't beˈlieve it. I'm ˈhopping ˈmad at this.

B: ˈWhatˈ is it?

A: My ˈname's ˈnot on the ˈpassenger ˈlist.

B: ˈWhat? That can't beˈ ˈtrue! I ˈmade your ˈbooking two ˈmonths ago.

A: The ˈstation superinˈtendent says he's been ˈordered to ˈcancel ˈall ˈbookings from ˈHyderabad.

B: We must comˈplain to the ˈGeneral ˈManager.

A: But ˈthat's no ˈgood. ˈEven if we comˈplain I ˈcan't get ˈon this ˈtrain. ˈWhat do I ˈdo?

B: Well, we must ˈmake ˈsure you ˈleave by the ˈnext train.

Dialogue 8

A: Did you ˈget the ˈproject proˈposal?

B: ˈNo, I ˈdidn't.

A: But I ˈsent it by ˈcourier.

B: It must have ˈreached ˈafter I ˈleft.

A: Oh, ˈno! ˈThat's no ˈuse. Now we ˈwon't be able to ˈmeet the ˈdeadline.

B: Oh, ˈcome on. ˈDon't be so pessiˈmistic. I'm ˈsure we ˈcan.

Dialogue 9

A: Have we ˈmet beˈfore?

B: ˈNo I ˈdon't ˈthink so. I'm Suˈdhir.

A: ˈHello, Suˈdhir. I'm ˈArchana. I live ˈnext ˈdoor.

B: I'm from ˈDelhi. I ˈwork here. My ˈoffice is near ˈBombay ˈCentral. Where do ˈyou work?

A: Oh, I ˈteach at Bomˈbay Uniˈversity.

C: ˈHello, ˈyou two. I'm ˈso ˈglad you ˈmade it. D'you ˈknow each ˈother?

B: We've ˈjust introˈduced ˈourselves.

C: ˈLovely! (pause) ˈPlease ˈhelp yourselves to a ˈdrink.

A and B: We ˈwill. ˈThanks.

Dialogue 10

A: ˈWelcome to ˈCruise. I ˈhope you'll ˈlike it here.

B: I'm ˈsure I ˈwill. It's ˈjust the ˈkind of ˈwork I ˈwanted.

A: We're ˈglad to ˈhave you. ˈYou're the ˈkind of ˈperson we ˈneeded for the ˈjob.

B: ˈThank you. I'm ˈeager to ˈstart straightaˈway.

A: ˈCertainly. (pause) ˈThis is your ˈworkstation. You have a ˈteam of ˈfour to asˈsist you.

B: ˈWhat ˈtime do we ˈstart ˈwork every ˈday?

A: Well, we ˈwork ˈflexi time—ˈeight ˈhours a ˈday.

B: That ˈsuits me ˈfine.

Dialogue 11

A: ˈWhere were you ˈall of ˈlast ˈweek? The ˈprincipal ˈsent for you ˈtwice.

B: I was ˈquite unˈwell.

A: ˈWhat ˈhappened?

B: It ˈstarted with a seˈvere ˈheadache. Then I ˈgot a ˈcold and ˈfever.

A: Did you ˈsee a ˈdoctor?

B: ˈYes.

A: ˈWhat was ˈwrong?

B: He ˈsaid I ˈhad the ˈflu.

A: Are you all ˈright now?

B: ˈYes, ˈthanks. I ˈfeel a ˈbit ˈweak though.

A: It ˈalways ˈtakes ˈtime to reˈcover from the ˈflu. I ˈhope you ˈfeel ˈstrong again ˈsoon.

B: ˈThanks again. (pause) I ˈthink I'll ˈgo and ˈsee the ˈPrincipal.

A: ˈYes, ˈdo. ˈBye.

B: ˈBye.

Dialogue 12

A: D'you ˈknow ˈShalini has a large colˈlection of ˈminiatures?

B: ˈDoes she? Have you ˈseen them?

A: We're ˈgoing to ˈsee them at an exhiˈbition.

B: ˈWhen?

A: Toˈmorrow ˈmorning. Would you ˈlike to ˈcome?

B: Oh, ˈno. ˈNot in the ˈmorning, ˈsurely. We'll ˈwaste the ˈwhole ˈday.

A: ˈNo, we won't. We'll be ˈback in a ˈcouple of ˈhours.

B: I don't ˈthink I can ˈmake it. (I) ˈHaven't got the ˈtime.

A: ˈNor do ˈwe. But we had to ˈmake time.

B: I ˈreally ˈdon't think I ˈcan. ˈThanks all the same. (pause) ˈHave ˈfun all of you.

A: ˈThanks.

Activity 9

Words generally stressed are nouns, adjectives, main verbs (except the verb 'be') adverbs, demonstratives, *Who* question words, the negative 'not' and auxiliary verbs when the shortened form of the negative 'not' is attached to them, 'yes' and 'no' because they stand for a whole utterance, and greetings.

Activity 10

Dialogue 7: In B's last utterance 'train' is unstressed because it occurs immediately after A has used the word, and the word 'next' needs to be made prominent.
Dialogue 10: A's third utterance: 'You have a team ...'
Dialogue 12: A's first utterance, 'Shalini has a large collection ...'
Dialogue 12: A's fifth utterance, 'but we had to make time'. Here the word 'time' occurs after B says 'Haven't got the time', where it is stressed. A does not stress 'time' because he wishes to focus on the word 'make', which gives us added information.
Dialogue 12: B in her utterance 'haven't got the time' wishes to focus on 'haven't' and therefore does not stress 'got', which would normally be stressed.

Look at the word got in the following utterances for example:
I've ˈgot a ˈlarge colˈlection of ˈstamps.
Have you ˈgot the answer to this ˈquestion?

Activity 11

Personal pronouns, articles, prepositions, conjunctions, auxiliary verbs and the 'be' verb (am, is, are, was, were) are generally not stressed.

Activity 12

can: Modal verbs (without the negative attached to them) are generally unstressed. In dialogue 1, 'can' occurs in the final position and is therefore stressed.
am: In dialogue 2, B's first utterance is stressed for emphasis.
you and I'll: In dialogue 3, 'you' and 'I'll' are stressed because they highlight the responsibility of 'you' versus 'I'.
can: In dialogue 8, 'can' is stressed in B's last utterance because it occurs in the final position. In dialogue 12, 'can' occurs in the final position in B's last utterance and is stressed.
is: In dialogue 7 'is' stressed for emphasis in B's first utterance.
will: In dialogue 9, in A and B's utterance, 'will' is stressed because it occurs in the final position. In dialogue 10, in B's first utterance, 'will' occurs in the final position of the first part and is stressed.

Activity 13

Words that are important for meaning, that is content words, are generally stressed and those that are not so important for meaning, that is structure words, are generally not stressed.

Activity 15

1. I don't think so	refer back to something that has been said and say you don't believe it is true
2. get on with	progress with one's work
3. Aorry?	Could you repeat what you said?
4. I don't get you	don't understand you
5. catch the 8 a.m.	take the train/bus leaving at 8 a.m.
6. making time	making an effort to find time
7. hopping mad	very angry
8. get on the train	board it
9. get a letter	receive it
10. Oh, come on	we know what you said isn't true
11. you made it	managed to reach/be present at

12. help yourself to	to take what you want of something, for example food
13. work station	cubicle in an office for an individual to work
14. flexitime	work a fixed number of hours per day/week but start and finish working according to our choice
15. have the flu	suffer from it

Activity 16

1. get

a. get something	buy, bring, obtain something
b. get a channel	receive a channel
c. get a newspaper, magazine	subscribe to a newspaper, etc.
d. get marks/a grade	achieve, be given marks
e. get used to, angry, bored	become used to, angry, bored
f. get to know	begin to know
g. get dirty	become dirty
h. get back something	take back / recover something

2. make

a. make a will	write a will
b. make movies	direct/produce movies
c. make tea/coffee/ breakfast/lunch	prepare/cook tea/breakfast, etc.
d. make do	manage
e. make something of your life	achieve something
f. make off with	steal something
g. make money	earn or gain money

3. do

a. do the flowers	arrange the flowers
b. do the soup	cook the soup
c. do the dishes	wash the dishes
d. do without (somebody/something)	manage without
e. do somebody out of	deprive somebody of something, prevent someone from getting something
f. do a sum or crosswords	solve a sum, etc.
g. do a trip	take a trip
h. do 14 km to a litre of petrol	travel 14 km

i. do a drawing, painting	make, produce a drawing, etc.
j. to do history or any subject	study/learn history, etc.

4. go

a. go through something	study/examine (carefully) something
b. go down * (sun or moon)	set
b. go down (ship)	sink
c. go by *	to pass (of time)
d. go into *	join an organisation for a career, for example navy, army or teaching
e. go over something	check something

5. look

a. look into	investigate
b. look out for somebody	watch out
c. look somebody up	visit
d. look through somebody	ignore
e. look through something	examine/read

ACTIVITY 19

– let's, it's what's, you're, I've, I'll, we'll, it's (it has), that's, I'm, we've, d'you, we're
– don't, shouldn't, can't, didn't, isn't, won't, haven't
The contracted forms of words contribute to the characteristic rhythm of English.

Of the contracted forms listed:

a. The main types in the first list are those in which the shortened forms of the auxiliary verbs, 'am', 'is' (or 'has'), 'are', 'will', 'had' (or 'would') and 'have' are attached to the pronouns 'I', 'he', 'they' and 'we'. Thus' we get 'I'm', 'I'll', 'I'd', 'I've', 'he's', 'they're', 'we're', 'we'll', 'we'd', 'they've', 'they'd' and 'they'll'.
b. The verb 'let's' is the short form of 'let us'. It is generally used in conversation to make a suggestion, e.g. 'Let's go to the beach.'
c. 'What's' is the question word to which the short form of the verb 'is' is attached. Question words such as 'what' and 'how' can have the weak form of 'is/has' attached to them. e.g. What's (is) he doing?
Where's (has) she gone?

---

* These phrases have other meanings as well. Look up the dictionary for those meanings.

d. The short, or weak, form of 'is' can also be attached to nouns, e.g., 'Radha's (is) not at home' or 'Radha's (has) gone out' and 'The cat's (has) drunk all the milk.'
e. The short form of the auxiliary verb 'do' is attached to 'you' in question forms in conversation e.g. 'D'you like to play tennis?'

In the second list while the auxiliary verbs retain their full form, the weakened form of the negative 'not' (i.e. *n't*) is attached to them. So we get *is+n't*, *are+n't*, *do+n't*, *should+n't*, *can+n't*, *did+n't*, *would+n't*, *will+n't* (*won't*), *have+n't* and *has+n't*.

Activity 21

The lack of correspondence between spelling and sound in English necessitates the use of phonetic symbols (based on the principle of one symbol–one sound) to indicate the pronunciation of symbols. In order to consult the dictionary for the pronunciation of words, we need to learn the value of each symbol, that is the sound it stands for.

In words with more than one syllable, one of the syllables is said with greater breath force. In other words, it is stressed. We need to consult the dictionary for stress on English words. The stress is fixed on each word and has to be learnt. In most learners' dictionaries, stress is indicated by an upright mark in front of and above the stressed syllable.

In speech, words that are important for meaning, that is, content words are generally stressed. Words that are not so important for meaning, that is, structure words are generally not stressed.

Sometimes in context, words that are normally stressed are not stressed, particularly when the same word occurs a second time immediately after its first occurrence. Also, 'has' and 'have' are not stressed even though they function as main verbs when they mean 'to possess'.

Sometimes in context, words that are normally not stressed (structure words) are stressed for emphasis or contrast, when they (auxiliary verbs) occur in the final position in utterances, and when they are attached to the weakened form of the negative 'not' (*n't*). The contracted and weakened forms of words in spoken English contribute to the characteristic rhythm of English.

PART

1

APPENDIX 3: NOTES AND PRACTICE MATERIALS ON PRONUNCIATION

As we have seen in Unit 5, dialogues can be used to teach listening for the pronunciation of words and the rhythm of English. The activities given below provide you with additional materials on the sounds of English, word stress and stress and rhythm in sentences (connected speech).

Look at the symbols for the consonant and vowel sounds along with a key word for each sound, and listen to them on the CD. These symbols are based on the principle of one symbol–one sound only and are given in the seventh edition of the Oxford Advanced Learner's Dictionary. They are used to indicate the pronunciation of words in the dictionary.

Consonants

To help you learn the symbols and the consonant sounds they stand for, look at each symbol, listen to the sound it represents on the CD and repeat the key word.

S. No.	*Phonetic symbol*	*Key word*
1.	p	pick
2.	b	bit
3.	t	tail
4.	d	dog
5.	k	kite

6.	g	get
7.	tʃ	chill
8.	dʒ	joy
9.	m	man
10.	n	note
11.	ŋ	thi<u>ng</u>
12.	f	fit
13.	v	vote
14.	θ	think
15.	ð	that
16.	s	send
17.	z	zone
18.	ʃ	shine
19.	ʒ	vision
20.	h	heat
21.	l	lake
22.	r	red
23.	j	yoke
24.	w	well

Activity 1

Listen to each word, write down the symbol for each consonant you hear, and put a dash for the vowel(s).
Example: *stiff: st – f*

1. brook
2. song
3. rise
4. peace
5. breathe
6. rice
7. sums
8. cough
9. judge
10. crown
11. think
12. chance
13. zinc
14. fruit
15. shelf
16. pleasure
17. machine
18. straight
19. debt
20. watch
21. receipt
22. quite
23. squash
24. swan
25. hive
26. ground

If you find some sounds difficult to produce (refer to Unit 5), here are a few exercises to help you learn the difference between pairs of sounds.

a. Consonants /p/ and /f/: For the production of /p/, we have to bring the lips together. For the production of /f/, the upper teeth must be placed lightly on the lower lip.
Listen to the following pairs of words on the CD and repeat them.

/p/	/f/
peas	fees
pig	fig
port	fort
reap	reef
pour	four
put	foot
peel	feel
pit	fit
pond	fond

If you need further practice in producing the consonant /f/, listen to the following words on the CD and repeat them.

/f/	/f/	/f/
fault	affair	leaf
fate	prefer	proof
fertile	refine	stiff
fever	refuse	grief
five	suffer	safe
fund	afford	laugh
photo	trophy	graph

b. Consonants /f/ and /v/: Listening to practise the distinction between the consonants /f/ and /v/ by the following words on the CD and repeating them.

/f/	/v/	/f/	/v/
feign	vain/vein	calf	carve
foil	voile	shelf	shelve
fine	vine	safe	save
fan	van	proof	prove
off	of	leaf	leave

For more practice in the consonant /v/, listen to the following words on the CD and repeat them.

/v/

valid	avoid	have
vein	invite	save
vegetable	review	believe
vigour	even	sieve

varnish	several	cave
variety	provoke	deprive

c. Consonants /v/ and /b/: If you find it difficult to maintain the distinction between these two consonants, listen to the following pairs of words on the CD and repeat them.

/v/	/b/
van	ban
vein	bane
veil	bale
vile	bile
voile	boil
vote	boat
very	bury/berry
vent	bent
vowel	bowel

d. Another distinction we may find difficult to maintain is the one between the consonants /s/ and /z/. Listen to the following pairs of words for practice.

/s/	/z/	/s/	/z/
seal	zeal	niece	knees
sue	zoo	peace/piece	peas
sink	zinc	cease	seize
sip	zip	loose	lose
dose	doze	bus	buzz
race	rays	fleece	fleas

e. Some of us find it difficult to maintain the distinction between the consonants /z/ and /dʒ/. For the production of /z/, we must raise the tip and blade of the tongue towards the teeth ridge (behind the upper teeth) so that there is a narrow passage between the ridge and the blade of the tongue, through which the air passes out continuously with friction. For the production of /dʒ/, on the other hand, a complete closure is made by the tongue against the teeth ridge and the hard palate, and then the tongue is lowered to let the air out very slowly.

Listen to the following words on the CD and repeat them for practise.

/z/		
zoo	leaves	breeze
zone	cousin	rose
zeal	possess	lose
zebra	puzzle	bees
zero	business	tease
z	deserve	size

/dʒ/

germ	adjust	bridge
judge	adjourn	cage
joke	budget	dodge
journey	suggest	siege
giraffe	injure	wage

Now listen to the following pairs of words distinguishing between /z/ and /dʒ/ and practise pronouncing them.

/z/	/dʒ/	/z/	/dʒ/
zoo	jew	buzz	budge
zealous	jealous	raise	rage
zest	jest	seize	siege
		ways	wage

f. We need to maintain the distinction between /s/ and /ʃ/ and /s/ and /tʃ/. Here are pairs of words that you could practise saying aloud if you find it difficult to maintain the distinction between them. Listen and repeat each pair.

/s/	/tʃ/	/s/	/tʃ/	/s/	/tʃ/
sell	shell	seek	check	sheet	cheat
self	shelf	sip	chip	share	chair
sign	shine	soak	choke	shin	chin
parcel	partial	seat	cheat	shoes	choose
seer	sheer	sill	chill	shop	chop
sip	ship	sore	chore	ship	chip
		hiss	hitch	dish	ditch
		lass	latch	lash	latch

Activity 2

g. Write down five words (other than the ones given above) to illustrate each of the following consonants s, tʃ, f, s, dʒ, z, v, w. Refer to the dictionary to check your answers.

Pronunciation of Suffixes

The plural and possessive forms of nouns and the third person singular forms of verbs (-s, -es, -'s, -s') are pronounced in the following three ways.

a. /ɪz/ after the consonant sounds /z, dʒ, s, ʃ, tʃ/.

Examples:

nouns		*verbs*	
horses	bushes	matches	curses, assesses
doses	garages	messages	abuses
roses	mirages	Raj's	closes
prizes	watches	Alice's	rushes
		Dicken's	brushes
			catches
			fetches
			merges

b. /z/ after the consonants /b, d, g, m, n, ð, v, l, ŋ/, vowel + /r/ and all vowels.

Examples:

nouns	*verbs*
herbs	grabs
sands	reads
bags	drags
games	rhymes
films	runs
signs	sings
rungs	believes
leaves	breathes
wreathes	expels
shells	goes
berries	roars
colours	sees
chairs	
John's	
man's	
China's	
employees'	

c. /s/ after /f, k, p, t and θ/

Examples:

nouns		*verbs*	
pups		Bert's	hops, skips
hats	giraffes	Dick's	fasts, packs
rocks	chiefs	Ruth's	bluffs, berths
	hearths		

The past suffix *–ed*, which changes the regular verbs into their past and past participle forms, is pronounced in three different ways.

a. /ɪd/ after the consonants /t and d/

Examples:

painted raided
haunted grounded
batted sounded
sorted padded

b. /t/ after the consonants /p, k, s, θ, tʃ, ʃ and f/

Examples:

stopped earthed
looked crossed
hatched brushed
coughed

c. /d/ after the other 11 consonants and all the vowels

Examples:

dubbed vowed
flagged delayed
stemmed sewed
turned stared
crowned banged
breathed judged
loved buzzed
camouflaged compelled

Vowels

In English, as also in other languages, a word is made up of two types of sounds: consonants and vowels. In English, every word must have a vowel sound, though it may or may not have a consonant sound. For example, the words *eye, ah, I,* have no consonant and only one vowel each. The words 'eat', 'elf', 'bridge', 'stream' have one, two, three and four consonants respectively in addition to one vowel each. As all these words have only one vowel, they consist of only one syllable. However, not all English words have only one syllable. In other words, many English words have more than one vowel and, therefore, more than one syllable. For example, the words 'passage' and 'sixteen' have two vowels each and, therefore, two syllables each: *pass+age, six+teen*. The words 'already' and 'disappoint' have three vowels and therefore three syllables each: *al+rea+dy, dis+ap+point*. The words 'integrity' and 'legitimate' have four vowel sounds and therefore four syllables each: *in+te+gri+ty, le+gi+ti+mate*. The words 'interrogative' and 'organisation' have five vowels and therefore five syllables each: *in+ter+ro+ga+tive, or+ga+ni+sa+tion*. The word 'responsibility' has six vowel sounds and therefore six syllables: *re+spon+si+bi+li+ty*. It is clear from these words that there are as many syllables in a word as there are vowel sounds. We shall refer to the syllable when we consider word stress in English.

Let us look at the symbols for the vowels, listen to the sound each symbol represents and repeat the keywords.

S. No.	*Phonetic symbol*	*Keyword*
1	iː	eat, neat, tea
2	ɪ*	it, knit, pin
3	e	edge, net
4	æ	add, flag
5	ɑː	ask, brass
6	ɒ	odd, knot, fox
7	ɔː	ought, talk, law
8	ʊ**	pull, wool
9	uː	food, route, blue
10	ʌ	luck, fun, sun
11	ɜː	earn, bird, stir
12	ə	above, forget, mother
13	eɪ	eight, grade, day
14	əʊ	own, goal, sew
15	aɪ	aisle, rhyme, buy
16	aʊ	out, brown, now
17	ɔɪ	oil, join, toy
18	ɪə	ear, beard, mere
19	eə	heir, scarce, stare
20	ʊə	fluent, gourd, pure

* *Advanced Learner's Dictionary* (7th edition) lists another vowel symbol /i/. This does not need to be learnt, because in its place we can use /ɪ/.

** *Advanced Learner's Dictionary* (7th edition) lists another vowel symbol /u/. This does not need to be learnt, because in its place we can use /ʊ/

You must have noticed that most of the vowel symbols are not letters of the Roman alphabet as used in English and are, therefore, not familiar. The second vowel in the above list is the small capital letter and not the capital 'I' we normally use. Similarly, the eighth vowel is not the capital letter 'U'. While the first component of the symbols for vowels 15 and 16 is the printed letter 'a', the symbol for vowel e is the letter 'a' we normally use in writing.

Notice that the vowels 13–20 have two symbols each. The two symbols indicate that in the production of these vowels the tongue moves from one position towards another. For example, the symbol /eɪ/ indicates that we start with the tongue in position for /e/ (ए in Hindi) and then move the tongue towards the position for the articulation of /ɪ/. Listen to these vowels again. Owing to the two movements of the tongue, these sounds are known as diphthongs.

We find some vowels difficult to produce because they do not exist in most Indian languages. These vowels are /e, æ, ɜː, ʌ, ɔː, eɪ, əʊ, ɪə, eə, ʊə, ɔɪ/. To acquire these and the other vowels, it is best to compare them with each other. Look at the pairs of words below, and listen to the difference between /iː/ and /ɪ/. Then repeat them. Remember that /iː/ is much longer than /ɪ/.

/ɪ/	/iː/	/ɪ/	/iː/	/ɪ/	/iː/
bit	beat	rid	read	ship	sheep
fist	feast	fill	feel	live	leave

Think of other similar pairs of words to distinguish between /iː/ and /ɪ/ and write them down.

We need to distinguish between /ɪ/ and /e/. Listen to the following pairs of words and repeat each pair.

/ɪ/	/e/	/ɪ/	/e/
hid	head	sit	set
knit	net	fill	fell
bliss	bless	middle	meddle/medal
rid	red	tin	ten

Write down other pairs of words to distinguish between /ɪ/ and /e/.

Another important distinction we need to maintain is between /e/ as in 'bed' and /æ/ as in 'bad'. Look at the following pairs of words, listen to them and repeat each pair.

/e/	/æ/	/e/	/æ/
bet	bat	merry	marry
said	sad	gem	jam
lend	land	mess	mass
kettle	cattle	net	gnat
men	man	wren	ran

We need to distinguish between /e/ as in 'let' and /eɪ/* as in 'late'. Listen to the following pairs of words and repeat each pair.

---

* In India, most of us pronounce this diphthong like the Hindi vowel ए and not like the British /eɪ/. Since our pronunciation is widely understood, we need not necessarily acquire the British pronunciation. However, we must maintain the distinction between this vowel and the vowel /e/.

/e/	/eɪ/ (or /e:/)	/e/	/eɪ/ (or /e:/)
red	raid	test	taste
men	main/mane	pepper	paper
tell	tale	hell	hail/hale
sent	saint	cellar	sailor

Some of us may find it a problem to distinguish between the vowel /ɑ:/ as in 'fast' and the vowel /ɜ:/ as in 'first'. Whereas for /ɑ:/ we need to open our mouth wide, for the production of / ɜ:/, the mouth should not be opened wide. Listen to the difference between the two sounds in the following pairs of words, and then repeat each pair.

/ɑ:/	/ɜ:/	/ɑ:/	/ɜ:/
farm	firm	shark	shirk
hard	heard	bath	birth
cast	cursed	father	further
guard	gird	lark	lurk
barn	burn	fast	first

The vowel /ɑ:/ as in 'last' must be distinguished from the vowel /b/ as in 'lost'. The main different between these two vowels is that for /ɑ:/ the lips are not rounded, whereas for /ɒ/ they are, although the rounding is slight. In addition, /ɑ:/ is perceptibly longer than /ɒ/. Listen to the difference between the two vowels in the following pairs of words. Then repeat each pair.

/ɑ:/	/ɒ/	/ɑ:/	/ɒ/
cast	cost	guard	god
dart	dot	sharp	shop
calf	cough	large	lodge
last	lost	mark	mock
heart	hot	card	cod

Another pair of vowels that need to be distinguished is /ɑ:/ as in 'card' and /ɔ:/ as in 'cord'. Most Indians do not use the vowel /ɔ:/ in 'caught' and 'bought'. Instead we use a relatively longer variety /ɒ/ as in 'cot'. Such substitution is acceptable only if /ɒ/ is made sufficiently long so that a clear distinction is maintained between /ɒ/ as in 'cot' and /ɔ:/ as in 'caught'. However, we have to take care not to use /ɑ:/ in place of /ɔ:/.

Listen to the difference between /ɑ:/ and /ɔ:/ in the following pairs of words and repeat them.

/ɑ:/	/ɔ:/	/ɑ:/	/ɔ:/
barn	born/borne	art	ought
cart	caught/court	tart	taught
darn	dawn	hark	hawk
hard	hoard	card	cord/chord

For the vowel /əʊ/, it is possible to use the vowel /o:/ (ओ) as in the Hindi word गोल because this is widely understood and therefore widely acceptable. But if we use this vowel in place of the vowel /ɒ/ as in 'hot', it would blur the distinction between them and therefore be unacceptable. Listen to the distinction between /ɒ/ and /əʊ/ in the following pairs of words and repeat each pair.

/ɒ/	/əʊ/	/ɒ/	/əʊ/
dot	dote	cod	code
got	goat	cost	coast
fond	phoned	hop	hope
rod	road	not	note
sock	soak	clock	cloak

Can you think of other pairs of words to distinguish between /ɒ/ and /əʊ/?
The vowel /u:/ is much longer than /ʊ/. If you find it difficult to distinguish between the two vowels, listen to the following words and repeat them. First, words with /u:/:

food	tune
rude	fruit
knew/new	group
spool	clue
tool	troop

Then words with /ʊ:/

foot	pull
sugar	book
woman	wool
wolf	courier
could	should

It is also important to maintain the distinction between /ɑɪ/ and /ɔɪ/. First, listen to each of the following words and fill in the blank space in each with the symbol for the sound you hear.

a.	pl	e.	str ....
b.	st	f.	l
c.	an	g.	l........tr
d.	k ......n	h.	f l

Now listen to the difference between the vowels /ɑɪ/ and /ɔɪ/ in the following pairs of words and repeat them.

/aɪ/	/ɔɪ/	/aɪ/	/ɔɪ/
buy	boy	vice	voice
file	foil	isle	oil

ply	ploy	bile	boil
tie	toy	tile	toil

Some of us find it difficult to produce the vowel /ʊə/ and tend to replace it with /u:/ in such words as 'tour', 'pure', 'poor', 'moor' and 'jury'. This is not acceptable in British English, though an alternative pronunciation of these words with the vowel /i:/ in place of /ʊə/ is acceptable.

If you find it difficult to produce /ʊə/, listen to the following words with the vowel sound and repeat them.

poor	dual	casual
tour	mature	manual
pure	jury	obscure
cure	endure	sure

Word stress

We have already seen that every word in English must have a vowel. It may or may not have a consonant. The number of vowels in a word determines the number of syllables in it. When a word has more than one vowel and, therefore, more than one syllable, one of the syllables is said with greater breath force and is therefore heard as louder than the other syllables. Thus, that syllable is said to be stressed. The stress in English words is fixed and has to be learnt.

1. Some English words of two syllables, have stress on the first syllable and others have the stress on the second syllable.
   Examples of words with stress on the first syllable:
   ˈalmost, ˈbargain, ˈgovern, ˈsurface, ˈinjure
   Examples of words with stress on the second syllable:
   adˈmit, beˈlieve, forˈbid, monˈsoon, miˈstake, surˈprise, preˈfer
2. Given below are examples of words of three syllables, with the stress on different syllables.

stress on the 1st syllable	*stress on the 2nd syllable*	*stress on the 3rd syllable*
ˈatmosphere	adˈventure	disapˈpoint
ˈrecipe	poˈtato	personˈnel
ˈfurniture	specˈtator	coinˈcide
ˈobstacle	exˈhibit	recolˈlect
ˈgovernment	umˈbrella	disapˈpear
ˈbadminton	deˈvelop	correˈspond
ˈcharacter		

3. Some examples of words of four syllables with the stress on different syllables, are given below.

stress on the 1st syllable	*stress on the 2nd syllable*	*stress on the 3rd syllable*	*stress on the 4th syllable*
ˈhonorary	reˈsponsible	panoˈrama	examiˈnee
ˈaristocrat	reˈpetitive	cataˈstrophic	
ˈmelancholy	comˈpetitive	appaˈratus	
ˈdefinitely	deˈmocracy	correˈspondence	
	adˈvertisement	inciˈdental	
	phoˈtography	matheˈmatics	
	conˈspiracy		
	conˈtemporary		

4. Finally, look at some examples of words of five syllables.

stress on the 1st syllable	*stress on the 2nd syllable*	*stress on the 3rd syllable*	*stress on the 4th syllable*
ˈfavouritism	iˈtinerary	anaˈlytical	acceleˈration
ˈsecularism		irreˈsponsible	environˈmental
		unaˈnimity	experiˈmental
		magnaˈnimity	

There are very few words of more than five syllables. For example, the word 'responsiˈbility' has six syllables. If we add the prefix, –ir then it has seven.

Notice that as words grow longer the stress tends to shift. Listen to the shift in stress on the following sets of words on the CD.

ˈdemocrat	deˈmocracy	demoˈcratic	democratiˈsation
ˈdiplomat	diˈplomacy	diploˈmatic	
ˈphoto	phoˈtography	photoˈgraphic	
ˈphotograph	phoˈtographer	photoˈgraphical	
	faˈmiliar	familiˈarity	familiariˈsation
ˈmechanism	meˈchanical	mechaˈnistic	mechaniˈsation
	eˈxamine		examiˈnation
ˈhypocrite	hyˈpocrisy	hypoˈcritical	
	aˈcademy	acaˈdemic	acadeˈmician
ˈallopath	alˈlopathy	alloˈpathic	
ˈhomeopath		homeˈopathy	homeoˈpathic
ˈpolitics	poˈlitical	poliˈtician	
	comˈpete	competeˈtition	
ˈgrammar	gramˈmatical	grammatiˈcality	

When you are not sure of the pronunciation of a word, look it up in the dictionary. Phonetic symbols are used to give the pronunciation of a word. Look at these and the stress mark on the stressed syllable and say the word aloud. Here are some common words. You could consult the dictionary for their pronunciation.

decay	between	attempt
agency	delicate	already
decision	determine	commentary
important	audition	delicious
introduce	represent	understand
educate	available	apostrophe
deliberate	aluminium	comprehend
controversial	peculiar	peculiarity
unanimous	vocabulary	

For more details on the vowels, the consonants, word stress and rhythm in English, refer to Sethi, Sadanand and Jindal: *A Practical Course in English Pronunciation*, New Delhi: Prentice-Hall of India Pvt. Ltd., 2004.

Stress and Rhythm in English

The characteristic rhythm of spoken English is a result of the way words that make up sentences are stressed in connected speech. Let us understand how this happens.

Sentence Stress

We have already pointed out (Unit 5, Appendix 2) that content words are generally stressed and structure words are generally not stressed in connected speech. There are exceptions to these rules in context. Content words are sometimes not stressed. For example, when a content word occurs a second time soon after its first occurrence, it is not stressed. The verb 'be' ('is', 'are', 'am') is not stressed except when it occurs in the final position in utterances, or is used for emphasis. Similarly, auxiliary verbs, which are generally not stressed, are stressed in the final position in utterances, or for emphasis or contrast. Prepositions, articles, conjunctions can also be stressed for the purpose of contrast, or for the purpose of highlighting them. Here are a few examples of these in context.

Dialogue 1

A: Is he ˈready?

B: ˈYes. He ˈis. / No. He ˈisn't.

DIALOGUE 2

A: ˈDon't ˈpunish him just this ˈonce.

B: I ˈam going to punish him. It'll ˈteach him a ˈlesson. This is the ˈthird ˈtime he's ˈdone this. (ˈ*am* for emphasis)

DIALOGUE 3

A: ˈIs that a ˈmessage from the ˈboss?

B: ˈNo. It's a message ˈto him. I'm going to ˈsend it to him. (ˈ*to* in contrast to *from*)

DIALOGUE 4

A: This is a ˈinteresting ˈstory. I ˈread it last ˈweek.

B: You ˈdon't say ‘ˈa interesting storyˈ, you say ‘ˈan interestingˈ story. Don't you reˈmember the ˈrule?

A: ˈYes, of course. You say ‘ˈan' and ‘ˈthe' before ˈvowels.

B: ˈThat's ˈright.

DIALOGUE 5

A: D'you ˈthink you can ˈsolve this ˈpuzzle?

B: Can I ˈtake a ˈlook?

A: ˈCertainly

B: ˈYes. I ˈthink I ˈcan. (Compare ‘can' with the word appearing in A's and B's first utterance.)

RHYTHM

We can acquire the rhythm of English if we take care to move from one stressed syllable to the next and weaken the unstressed syllables between two stressed syllables. In most weakened syllables, the vowel /e/ is used. For example, in the words ‘aˈbove', ‘ˈsecond' and ‘colˈlect', *a* /e/, *o* /e/ and *o* /e/ are all unstressed syllables.

Similarly, structure words generally also have a weak vowel (mostly /e/). For example:

articles:	*weak forms*
‘a' /eI/	/e/
‘an' /cen/	/en/
‘the' /ri:/	/de/
prepositions:	
‘for' /fe/	/fe/
‘from' /from/	/frrm/

'at' /aet/	/et/
'of', 'to' /bv, tu:/	/dv, te/ (before consonants) /tu/ (before vowels)
conjunctions:	
and, as, than /aend, aez, daen/	/end (en, n), ez, den/
that, but /daet, bvt/	/det, bet/
auxiliary verbs	*weak forms*
am, are, is /aem, a:, Iz/	/dm, e, z/s/
was, were, do /wbz, w3:, du:/	/wez, we, d (as in 'd' you)
does, had, has /dnz, haed, haez/	/dez, hed, hez/
have, can, could /haev, kaen, kvd/	/hav (av, v), k(g)n, ked/
shall, should, must /Sael, Sud, mvst/	/S(e)l, Sed, mest/
would /wud/	/wedld (as in 'I'd)
will /wIl/	/l (as in 'we'll', 'they'll')
be, been /bi; bI:n/	/bI, bIn/

The introductory 'there' is pronounced /de/ before consonants and /der/ before vowels. For example, look at these two sentences below and listen to them.

There must not be any gaps here. /de/
There aren't any examples of this /der/
'There is' is pronounced /dez/

Listen to some of these weak forms and contracted forms in the following sentences on the CD. While you listen, make a note of how the speaker links the ends and beginnings of words. These are marked with curved lines. Do remember to stress the syllables that have stress marks before them.

Don't for'get to 'phone them.
You must 'go to them as soon as you 'can.
It's 'easier than I 'thought it 'was.
Can 'Arjun 'help us 'sort out this 'problem?
I should (h)ave in'vited them for a 'game of 'tennis.
There's an 'urgent 'message from a 'client.
We've 'had 'rough 'weather through'out the 'week.
Does she 'like 'Indian or Chi'nese 'food.
If we'd 'informed them 'earlier, they'd (h)ave 'come in 'time.
'One 'bottle of 'water 'isn't e'nough for all of us.
We're 'going on an ex'cursion at the week'end.
There's such a 'lot of 'work 'pending that all of them are under tremendous pressure.
They'll 'have to 'find a so'lution to this by the end of the 'month.
The 'illustrations in this encyclo'paedia have been 'carefully 'done.
Her per'formance is 'proof of her 'talent as an 'actress.

Let us recapitulate the three features that characterise the rhythm of English:

1. There is a more or less regular occurrence of stressed syllables (in words) in an utterance with varying numbers of unstressed syllables between them.
2. The syllables that are not stressed are weakened, and some structure words (such as auxiliary verbs) are shortened or contracted as in *I've*, *we've* and *would've* (where 'have' is contracted), *we'll* and *they'll* (where 'will' is contracted), *we'd*, *they'd* and *I'd* (where 'had' is contracted), *she's*, *he's* and *it's* (where 'is' is contracted), and *we're* and *they're* (where 'are' is contracted). The negative 'not' is shortened as in *couldn't*, *can't*, *wouldn't*, *shan't* (shall not), *aren't* and *weren't*.
3. Consonants at the ends of words are linked with the vowels at the beginnings of words that follow them. For example, in the sentence 'One bottle of water isn't enough for all of us', the *le* in 'bottle' links with the *o* in 'of', the *r* at the end of 'water' links with the *i* in 'isn't', the *t* at the end of 'isn't' links with the *e* in 'enough', the *r* at the end of 'for' links with the *a* of 'all', the *l* of 'all' links with the *o* of 'of'; and the *f* in 'of' links with the *u* in 'us'. Thus, the sentence sounds like this:
   wʌn bɒtləv wɔ:tərɪzn tɪnʌf fərɔ:l əvəs

PART 1

APPENDIX 4: TRANSCRIPTS

Unit 2

TRANSCRIPT 1

The shock of yet another hit-and-run case.

A sixteen-year-old boy taken into custody by the police. The shocking part is the boy was accused of ramming into and killing five members of a family including three children may just be let off with a fine of a ₹ 1000. This is a time when Delhi police is claiming a crack down on under-age driving. Kurshid with the details:

The Gargs are inconsolable. The tears have now given way to anger and frustration. The family wants justice.

Meanwhile the sixteen-year-old, accused of being at the wheel of the Scorpio, was produced in a juvenile court on Monday. His judicial custody has been extended till the 24th of December. Brahm Prakash Chaudhary, the father of the accused and the owner of the Scorpio, could get away with a fine of as little as ₹ 1000. That's because the Delhi police had slapped the Motor Vehicles Act on him and not held him accountable for culpable homicide.

'We have registered a case under Section 279 and 304 IPC, and the boy has been booked under those provisions of IPC and regarding the father, he's liable under Motor Vehicle Act.' Legal experts have come forward in the criticism of the Delhi police for the way they've handled the case.

'It leaves the civil society aghast that they would contradict themselves by charging the father under 180 and then forget the ingredients of 180 and 304 part 2 being the same.' Senior police officials have told the CNN-IBN off camera that provisions of the relevant Motor Vehicles Act have been for the Delhi police to take strict action against the accused. Meanwhile the boy has been charged for rash and negligent driving and culpable homicide not amounting to murder. But being a juvenile, if convicted, he'll be sent to an observation home and not a prison. With bureau inputs in New Delhi, this is Rahi Khurshid.

Transcript 2

And now our special series.

A question on environment? I know we had a question on the environment.

A: While travelling through some parts of India, I've experienced personally the poor and poverty and seen all the glittering within India. And how do you change the country in terms of having a more environmental focus and mindset when most of India are just struggling to survive?

B: But it's a big challenge because on one side you see development and on the other side you see the degradation of the environment. So these two things have to be balanced out and it's not just air, we're looking at water, we're looking at noise, we're looking at all kinds of er... pollution er... that're... that are happening. But what's been put in place is that now you have er... environmental impact assessments done for large projects before they get executed. So that is a positive step. But that's confined only to the urban areas.

C: Even after they start and they're midway through and then the court will suddenly come up and say all right stop work.

B: Yes, of course, there are some projects which go through intense scrutiny before they are actually put in place, environmental scrutiny included. On the other side, there are so many projects across the country which are just going on for political will or whatever other reasons which are absolutely absent of this kind of scrutiny. So what we need is a comprehensive policy which is spreading all across the country for all scale of projects and that will make sure that development takes place but also environment is not sacrificed.

Unit 3

Transcript 1

The sale of the *Junta* during the month of January was rather poor. On the whole only 100 copies got sold. The number of copies sold of the paper *Events*, on the other hand, exceeded the number of copies of the *Junta* by twenty.

In February, the sale of the the *Junta* dropped by ten and so did the sale of *Events*. However, in March, there was a marked improvement in the sales of the *Junta*, that is, a hundred more than in February whereas the sale of *Events* dropped by twenty. In April, the sales of both the newspapers shot up, and while the *Junta* sold 300 copies, *Events* sold 350 copies. In May, a major sales campaign drive was organised by the managements of both the papers. The campaign was extremely successful and led to a tremendous improvement in the sales.

The sales doubled. While the *Junta* declared that they had sold 600 copies of the paper, *Events* sold 700 copies. In June, the sales of both the papers did not show any remarkable difference. The two dailies sold 620 and 710 copies respectively.

TRANSCRIPT 2

Here is an opportunity for you to experience the peace and calm that you can derive from a breathtaking view of the mountains in Himachal Pradesh and Kashmir, the serenity of the backwaters of Kerala, and the awesome beauty of the forests and the animals that inhabit them.

We, Crystal Travel and Tours, offer tour packages at a discount—at very competitive rates, and ensure that you enjoy your holiday.

The tour packages to the North of the country include one to Himachal Pradesh and another to the Kashmir Valley.

In Himachal Pradesh, two of you can visit Shimla, Manali and Kullu and spend 5 nights and 6 thoroughly enjoyable days for just ₹ 21,000, which will include accommodation with breakfast and sightseeing. The tour will start from Kalka.

The 6-night and 7-day tour to the Kashmir valley includes visits to Srinagar, Pahalgam, Gulmarg and back to Srinagar. The two- or three-star accommodation for two includes breakfast. But during the overnight stay in a houseboat, all your meals will be on the house and a car is at your disposal for all sightseeing. All this for only ₹ 29,999!

Another quite different tour package that we offer is the Kerala backwater tour package for 3 nights and 4 days to Cochin, Munnar and Alleppey. We provide three-star accommodation which includes breakfast. However, your stay in a houseboat would be inclusive of all meals. And all this for only ₹ 16,000.

If you find wildlife fascinating, the ideal tour to take would be our Corbett wildlife tour from Ramnagar for 2 nights and 3 days. The cost would be just ₹ 6,000 which includes accommodation for two with breakfast, pick up and drop at Ramnagar railway station.

We have other attractive offers as well and assure you of excellent service at affordable rates. For further information call us on 09833460173 or 09865400028 or e-mail us at info@crystaltandt.com.

Unit 4

TRANSCRIPT 1

International Women's Day Conclave

Panel Discussion: Know Your Right

Anchor: Hello. I'm Swapna Chidambaram.

I would like to welcome all of you on behalf of the CNBC team and IMC ladies wing.

What are your rights as a daughter, as a mother, as a wife, as a working woman specially when it comes to critical issues like child custody, inheritance, divorce, abuse and alimony. To address some of these issues, we have five panellists.

Our first panellist today is Purvi Chutani. Purvi is a lawyer and her areas of practice include cross-border immigration issues and adoption issues that affect families, children and women.

Our next panellist is Shobha Jagtiani. Shobha specialises in issues related to inheritance, succession and taxation.

Our third panellist is Supreme Court advocate, Rani Jethmalani. Rani is an activist and deals with issues related to domestic violence and abuse.

We have artist Kahini Merchant. Kahini is a painter and she's also the Executive Director of Merchant Media.

And our fifth panellist today is Satya Sagar. Satya is the editor of the women's magazine *Need* from DNA.

Shobha, could you tell us something about what is it we need to know about what we are entitled to as women when there is a will or when there is no will?

Shobha:Under the Indian Constitution, we have guaranteed to us the freedom of religion and the freedom to be governed by our personal laws. So the answer really depends on whether you are daughter in a Hindu family, a Muslim family, Parsi, Christian, Jew, etc. The Hindu Succession Act guarantees that the daughter will get an equal share, equal to that of the son. So there's no distinction between a daughter and son. However, this really applies to what is known as individual property of the father that passes on to the children. Up to 2005, the law in India was that as far as Hindu undivided family property what is known as coparcenary property, is concerned, a daughter had no share as far as an all India law was concerned. However, I might add that some states took the very progressive step, and in Maharashtra since 1994 we had an amendment that a daughter had rights equal to that of a son even in Hindu undivided family property. Now as far as Muslims are concerned, it's well known that under the Shariat Act, a daughter gets a share which is equal to half that of her brother, and even by will that cannot be completely remedied because under the Muslim law only er... two-third of the property er... one third of the property can be bequeathed under a will, whereas under Hindu law the entire property can be given away under a will by a testator, which means this that if a father wants to disinherit his daughter completely, he can do so by making a will.

Anchor: Okay. What about if you have an... er... adopted child you know, then what are your rights in that case? Purvi, can you er... throw some light on that?

Purvi: If you are adopted under the Hindu... Hindu law, then the child has got full inheritance right. But if you have... if you've adopted two children of the same sex then er... that is not allowed actually, but one would be under the Hindu Act, and the second one would be under the Guardian and Wards Act. And the child that is adopted under the Guardian and Wards Act doesn't get full inheritance rights. So the way to protect the child would be only by will. That has to be kept in mind when adopting two children of the same sex.

Well one could see this is given by law

Anchor: What happens when a will is contested? Suppose er... you know a son and a daughter are given equal portions by... in the will, and the son says you know I don't think this is her right, it's mine because of various reasons. What happens then?

Is a probate then perhaps ...?

Shobha:Then we have to see whether the will is valid, and that brings us to a very important topic. What are the ingredients of a valid will? It's very simple to make a valid will, it's not difficult at all. Er... the only requirements are, that the will must be made by a person of sound mind who is not labouring under any mental disability. Then there should be two witnesses to the will. The will need not be registered, it need not be in any legal language or format. And the will must have executors appointed under the will to see that the directions under the will are carried out.

Anchor: Shobha, so what you're saying is that if we have a valid will, then it follows that the son cannot contest it. The son cannot then make a claim saying that only he is entitled to the property and not the daughter. Have you come across any instances when people are not getting maintenance and support from their husbands? And what is it that you know they have done to get recourse under law?

A lot of people writing in perhaps to you ...

Shobha:No, I would actually go deeper into the problem and say that you can be a husband and wife living in the same home and because of whatever reason being denied the right you have as an individual. That is, if there is a certain amount of er... you know you are not given the money that you need to run the house properly, you're not given spending money, I think it starts from there, the right to be treated as an equal starts from there, and I would like to know if there is any provision besides what is in the letter of law that can enforce that a person has full right as a matter of fact.

Anchor: Even within the legal framework, what is it that one is entitled to?

Rani: I think there's a broad provision under the constitution of the right to equality and equality before the law. So I think anything that you can agitate ultimately you'll go to the highest law to agitate it. Even the question of er... you know, women when they came to the courts, in the whole area of property which Shobha will of course elaborate on. We gradually got work rights slowly because we've used the constitutional provisions of equality but after the constitution is enacted, you can't say that a widow has a limited state. She has to have an absolute state. You can't say that a woman can't be a coparcener. Now every daughter is entitled to be coparcener in the coparcenary property.

Unit 5

Dialogue 1

A: Let's cross the bridge as quickly as we can.

B: You must be joking. It's quite dangerous to cross it. The river's flowing above the danger mark.

A: I don't think so. It shouldn't be a problem if we cross over immediately.

B: All right. Since you're so confident we might as well.

Dialogue 2

A: You look rather upset.

B: I am upset. I just can't get on with my work.

A: Why? What's the matter?

B: There are too many interruptions.

A: What about putting up a 'Do not disturb' sign on your door?

B: Good idea.

Dialogue 3

A: I've got to decide by this evening.

B: Sorry? I didn't get what you said. Decide what?

A: Where I should take the children on Sunday.

B: Didn't you say you were going to the zoo?

A: Yes. But many of the children would prefer to go to the circus.

B: Then we'll divide them into two groups. You can go with one group, and I'll go with the other. Get me?

A: Thanks a lot.

Dialogue 4

A: We'll have to hurry if we want to catch the 8 a.m. bus to the university.

B: Don't worry. There's plenty of time.

A: But we've got to wait for the others.

B: We don't have to. We can leave a message. Tell them we're on our way.

A: Oh, there they are. Now we can all leave together.

Dialogue 5

A: How did you like it?

B: Fascinating! It's always a pleasure to listen to him.

A: He makes it all sound so simple.

B: Just what we'd expect of an expert.

A: He's an exceptionally good speaker, isn't he?

B: (There's) No doubt about it.

Dialogue 6

A: Well, it's been so nice talking to you.

B: Thanks, for making time to see me.

A: (My) Pleasure. I wonder what the time is?

B: Er... It's nearly twelve.

A: Twelve! Already! I must hurry, or I'll miss my flight. Bye, bye.

B: Bye, and thanks again.

Dialogue 7

A: I just can't believe it. I'm hopping mad at this.

B: What is it?

A: My name's not on the passenger list.

B: What? I can't believe it! I made your booking two months ago.

A: The station superintendent says he's been ordered to cancel all bookings from Hyderabad.

B: We must complain to the general manager.

A: But that's no good. Even if we complain I can't get on this train. What do I do?

B: Well, we must make sure you leave by the next train.

Dialogue 8

A: Did you get the project proposal?

B: No, I didn't.

A: But I sent it by courier.

B: It must have reached after I left.

A: Oh, no! That's no use. Now we won't be able to meet the deadline.

B: Oh, come on! Don't be so pessimistic. I'm sure we can.

Dialogue 9

(At a party)

A: Have we met before?

B: No, I don't think so. I'm Sudhir.

A: Hello, Sudhir. I'm Archana. I live next door.

B: I'm from Delhi. I work here. My office is near Bombay Central. Where do you work?

A: Oh, I teach at the University of Mumbai.

C: Hello, you two. I'm so glad you made it. D'you know each other?

B: We've just introduced ourselves.

C: Lovely! (pause) Please help yourselves to a drink.

A and B: We will. Thanks.

Dialogue 10

A: Welcome to Cruise. I hope you'll like it here.

B: I'm sure I will. It's just the kind of work I wanted.

A: We're glad to have you. You're the kind of person we needed for the job.

B: Thank you. I'm eager to start straightaway.

A: Certainly. (pause) This is your workstation. You have a team of four to assist you.

B: What time do we start work every day?

A: Well, we work flexitime—eight hours a day.

B: That suits me fine.

Dialogue 11

A: Where were you all of last week? The principal sent for you twice.

B: I was quite unwell.

A: What happened?

B: It started with a severe headache. Then I got a cold and fever.

A: Did you see the doctor?

B: Yes.

A: What was wrong?

B: He said I had the flu.

A: Are you all right now?

B: Yes, thanks. I feel a bit weak though.

A: It always takes time to recover from the flu. I hope you feel strong again soon.

B: Thanks again. (pause) I think I'll go and see the principal.

A: Yes, do. Bye.

B: Bye.

Dialogue 12

A: D'you know Shalini has a large collection of miniatures?

B: Does she? Have you seen them?

A: We're going to see them at an exhibition.

B: When?

A: Tomorrow morning. Would you like to come?

B: Oh, no! Not in the morning surely. We'll waste the whole day.

A: No, we won't. We'll be back in a couple of hours.

B: I don't think I can make it. (I) Haven't got the time.

A: Nor do we. But we had to make time.

B: I don't think I can. Thanks all the same. (pause) Have fun all of you.

A: Thanks.

APPENDIX 5: SAMPLE MATERIALS

Unit 2

CLASSES 1/2/3

Listen carefully to a poem. While you listen, look at the poem in your book/on the blackboard.

I Walk
(*Gul Mohar Reader 1*: Teacher's Edition)

Frogs jump,
Caterpillars hump,
Worms wriggle,
Bugs jiggle,
Rabbits hop,
Horses clop,
Snakes slide,
Seagulls glide,
Mice creep,
Deer bounce,
Kittens pounce,
Lions stalk,
But
I walk.

Listen to the poem again and specially to the words that are underlined.

Activity 1 (Group work)

Now listen to the first two lines and write down the two words that sound alike. (Ans: *jump, hump*)

Activity 2

Listen to the poem again. As you listen, in column 2 write down the words that sound like the words in column 1.

Column 1		**Column 2**
(a) jump	Ans:	*hump*
(b) wriggle		*jiggle*
(c) hop		*clop*
(d) slide		*glide*
(e) bounce		*bounce*
(f) stalk		*walk*

There is one word in column 1 that has no word that sounds like it in the poem. Which word is it? (Ans: *creep*)

Activity 3

In column 1 the names of the creatures in the poem are given. In column 2 write down the word used to tell us how each one moves about from one place to another. For example, frogs: *jump*.

Column 1	**Column 2**
(a) frogs	*jump*
(b) caterpillars	*hump*
(c) worms	*wriggle*
(d) bugs	*jiggle*
(e) horses	*clop*
(f) deer	*bounce*
(g) seagulls	*glide*
(h) mice	*creep*
(i) lions	*stalk*
(j) kittens	*pounce*

Activity 4 (Group work)

Write down the title of the poem and the last line of the poem. Who does 'I' stand for? How do 'I' move about? Pick out the word that tells us that what a human being does to move about is different from what other creatures (animals, birds, insects, reptiles, etc.) do.

Activity 5

Now read the poem aloud.

Classes 3/4

(*Gul Mohar Reader 1*: Teacher's Edition)

b. Listen to a poem.

Twenty froggies went to school,
Down beside a rushy pool,
Twenty little coats of green,
Twenty vest all white and clean.
'We must be in time,' said they,
'First we study, then we play
That is how we keep the rule,
When we froggies go to school.'

c. Here is a dialogue Raghu has with animals.

Raghu is talking to some small animals. Listen to the conversation carefully. While you listen, look at some words/expression on the blackboard. Also look at the pictures of the animals Raghu is talking to.

(*Gul Mohar Reader 2*)

Raghu: Mouse, you're small. How d'you escape from big animals?
Mouse: That's easy! I hide in a hole in the ground.

Raghu: Hello, porcupine, what do you do when there's danger?
Porcupine: I have sharp quills all over my body.

Raghu: Tortoise, you're very slow. How d'you protect yourself?
Tortoise: I have a hard shell over my body. If a dog or a fox comes near me, I just pull my whole body under my shell and I'm quite safe.

Raghu: Octopus, you have a small soft body. Can I touch you?
Octopus: Don't! My long arm will lash you like a whip!

Raghu: What happened to your tail, lizard?
Lizard: I left it behind because someone tried to catch me by it.

Raghu: But how can you live without it?
Lizard: That's not a problem. It'll grow again.

PICTURES OF ANIMALS

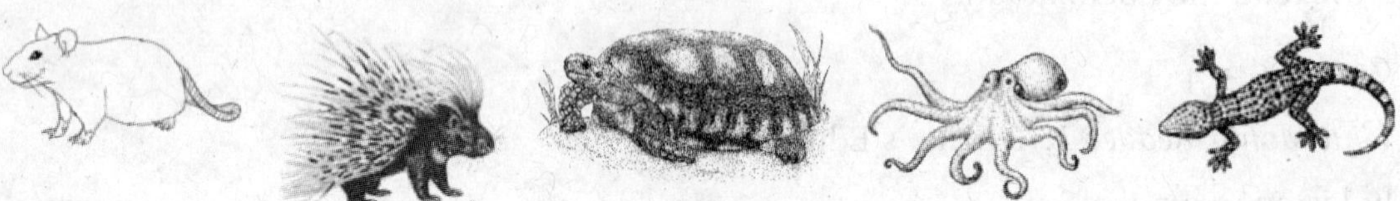

WORDS AND EXPRESSIONS

small animals escape from big animals,
there's danger,
protect yourself from

mouse	hide	hole
porcupine	stick out	quills
tortoise	pull	under shell
octopus	arms	lash, whip
lizard	leave behind	tail

ACTIVITY 1 (GROUPS OF 5 OR 6)

Listen to the conversation again and pick out three phrases that tell us what Raghu asks the small animals. Then one member of your group must tell the other groups what the conversation is about in one sentence.
(The teacher writes the sentences on the blackboard.)

ACTIVITY 2

Look at the words or expressions in column 1 below and match each of them with its meaning in column 2.

Column 1	*Column 2*	
a. escape from	hit with great force	*d*
b. there's danger	long and sharp pointed parts like needles	*f*

c. protect	a long piece of rope or leather attached to a handle	*e*
d. lash	let them stand upright	*g*
e. whip	make sure that someone is not harmed	*c*
f. quills	face some harm that might be done	*b*.
g. stick them out	get away from	*a*

Activity 3 (Groups of 6)

Each member of your group must play one of the roles—of Raghu and the five animals. Enact the dialogue for the other groups. You could exchange roles and enact the dialogue again.

Unit 3

Classes 1/2

Listen to the teacher's instructions and carry them out one by one.

Activity 1

Could you open the window and switch on the fan, please.

Activity 2

Open your books and turn to page ....

Activity 3

Look at the pictures on page ....

Activity 4

Listen to the teacher call out the name of each animal.

Activity 5

Tick the picture of the animal that your teacher calls out.

1. 2. 3. 4. 5. 6. 7. 8. 9. 10. 11.

a. horse	g. cock/hen	m. elephant
b. cow	h. rabbit	n. giraffe
c. dog	i. mouse	o. lion
d. buffalo	j. pig	p. tiger
e. cat	k. sheep/goat	q. monkey
f. parrot	l. bear	r. deer
		s. wolf
		t. fox

These activities can be linked to the speaking activities that follow.

Activity 6

The teacher will point to the picture of one of these animals. The student picked by the teacher must say what it is called.

Activity 7

Go to the blackboard. You will hear the teacher call out the name of one of these animals. Write down the name of the animal.

Activity 8 (Groups of 6)

The teacher writes down the names of each of the animals (in duplicate) on separate chits. Each group takes six chits. Then they read the name of the animal in the chit aloud. The group that reads the most words correctly wins.

Note: These activities can be repeated using lists of birds, flowers, fruits, vegetables, colours, etc.

Classes 4/5

Activity 1

Listen carefully to the instructions on how to make lime juice and watch your teacher carrying them out.

- First, pour water into a glass.
- Then add one and a half teaspoons of sugar to the water. Stir it till the sugar dissolves.
- After that cut the lime in half, squeeze it into the water and stir it.
- Then use a teaspoon to taste the lime juice. Is the sugar right? If it isn't, add some more.

- Finally, drink the lime juice and enjoy it.

To the teacher: This sample can be used to help students:
a. learn to follow instructions
b. use linkers in a sequence—first, then, after that, finally.
c. use the base form of the verb to give instructions
d. learn the pronunciation of words: *juice, pour, water, glass, teaspoons, sugar, dissolves, squeeze, half, drink, enjoy*

Take this listening exercise forward and link to speaking. Give students instructions (steps) on how to make tea or coffee or on how to draw a square or a rocket. Help the students use their imagination and give instructions to their classmates on how to make/draw things that they are good at (shapes with paper; object/animals with clay, figures, objects, etc.).

Classes 6/7/8

Activity 1

Look at the following words (can be written on the blackboard) while you listen to a passage on the CD.

chessmen	chessboard
pawns	squares
pieces	files
rooks (castles)	vertical columns
bishops	horizontal rows
a queen	ranks
a king	lettered

Chess is a game for two players. The players play with thirty-two white and black chessmen. Each of them has sixteen chessmen. These include eight pawns and eight pieces. Pawns are like common soldiers. The pieces consist of two rooks (also called castles), two knights, two bishops, a queen and a king.

A chessboard is used to play this game. It is made of cardboard and has the shape of a big square with sixty-four black and white small squares, arranged so that it looks like a black and white check, that is, no two squares next to each other are of the same colour. The square at the bottom left hand corner should be a black one and the square at the bottom right hand corner is white. The horizontal rows of squares are called 'files'. They are lettered from left to right a, b, c, d, e, f, g and h. The vertical columns of squares called 'ranks' are numbered 1 to 8 from the bottom upwards. So each square at the bottom has a number beginning with 'a1' at the left corner and ending with 'h1' at the right hand corner. Each square at the top has a number beginning with 'a8' at the left hand corner and 'h8' at the right hand corner.

Activity 2

Listen to the passage again and say what it is about. Tick the words in the list above that provided you with some clues.

Activity 3

Listen to the first part of the passage for answers to the following questions.

a. What is chess?
b. How many players are required to play chess?
c. What do the players use to play chess? How many of these are there altogether?
d. What are pawns? How many of them are there in all?
e. What are pieces? How many of them are there in all?
f. What do the pieces consist of? (two rooks, two knights, etc.)
g. How many pawns and pieces does each player have?

Activity 4

The answers to the questions above tell us what is required to play a game of chess. Now, listen to the second part of the passage about what a chessboard looks like. As you listen, make a note of the details mentioned.

To the teacher:

- a big square
- 64 black and white small squares
- square at bottom left, black
- square at bottom right, white
- horizontal rows, left to right, a to h
- vertical columns, bottom upwards, 1 to 8

Activity 5

a. What does 'horizontal rows' mean? Listen for a clue to its meaning (left to right).
b. What does 'vertical columns' mean? Can you guess the meaning from clue provided in the text (from the bottom upwards)?

Activity 6 (Groups of 6)

On the basis of your notes draw a chessboard, mark each square (a1, b1, c1, etc.) beginning with the bottom row, and go up to a8, b8, c8 etc., beginning at the top left hand corner.

To the teacher: You may link this activity to speaking by using the following activities in class. Start by asking how many students know how to play chess. Then have at least one student who is familiar with the game in each group.

ACTIVITY 7 (GROUPS OF 6)

If you know how to play chess, tell the others in the group how the game is played. You could begin like this:
In a game of chess there are two players. Each player has 8 pawns and 8 pieces. He/she can move his/her pieces forward and backward, but the pawns can only move forward. They cannot go back ....

(The infinitive forms of verbs such as *move, are, has, attack, go, save, capture, arrest* (movement), *warn* (opponent) and *escape* would probably occur in a description of how the game is played.)

ACTIVITY 8

Students who know how to play chess may take turns to explain how the game is played.

To the teacher: Put the verbs up on the blackboard. Point out that third person singular forms are different. For example:
Each player has (have) ...
Each player saves (save) ...
If a player captures ... it is removed ...
As player must try to capture the opponent's king...
The 'to' infinitive, on the other hand is the same for all the forms—first, second and third person singular and plural. Now you can move on to the next activity that focuses on the base form of verbs.

ACTIVITY 9

a. Look at the list of 'doing' words below. Use them in sentences. Put the sentences up on the blackboard.

play	bat	score
kick	try	attack
run	move	win
catch	bowl	lose
jump	protect	
hit	field	

b. Use some or all of these doing words to describe to the class how your favourite game is played. You could proceed in the following manner:
   - mention the name of your favourite game
   - what is required to play the game, e.g. field, ball, bat, net, rackets, shuttle cock, etc.
   - number of players required to play the game
   - the roles of the players in the game
   - the rules of the game
   - what the player(s) need(s) to do to win the game.

Note: The activities are progressively advanced and therefore not all of them need to be attempted by those classes that have English as a second language. The first five activities are comparatively easier than the last four activities. The teacher could select the activities according to the level of proficiency in English of their class.

CLASSES 7/8/9

ACTIVITY 1

Listen to information about the percentage of population by age-range in India for the year 2000 and the projected population in 2050 and fill in the chart below.

Year	*Age range*	*Percentage*
2000		
2050		

To the teacher: It is possible to use this chart for lower as well as higher classes. It could be left entirely blank for students from standards 8/9 and they could be asked to fill in the age range and also the percentage of population. For students with a lower level of proficiency part of the information could be filled in and the student asked to fill in the other half.

POPULATION SIZE

The world's population was growing at an alarming rate and doubled in the second half of the twentieth century, passing 6 billion. Though the rate of growth has slowed down in the world's two most populous countries—India and China, current trends indicate that the total population of the world will pass the 9 billion mark by 2050.

In the year 2000, the percentage of population in India was estimated at 7% in the age range of 60 years and above and 17% in the age range of 40–59 years. In the younger age groups, that is 20–39 years, it was 32%, and citizens in the age group up to 19 years comprised the highest at 44%.

In 2050, on the other hand, it is the percentage of senior citizens that is expected to increase to 20%—a 13% increase, and the population of people in the age group 40–50 will also increase by 9% to 26%. And a decrease in the population of younger people is expected. In the age group 20–39 years, there is likely to be a fall in the percentage of population from 32% to 27%, and in the age group up to 19 years, it will be reduced from 44% to 27%.

Thus it is indicated that as the population of the younger age groups gradually declines the population of older people or senior citizens is expected to rise.

Activity 2 (Groups of 6)

Listen to the information on population and age again and make a note of how the following words are pronounced. Notice that these words are pronounced differently when they function as nouns and when they function as verbs.

increase (verb)
decrease (verb)
increase (noun)
decrease (noun)

Can you think of other words that function as nouns, or adjectives and also as verbs? Look at the following words and listen carefully to their pronunciation both as nouns/adjectives and as verbs. Listen to the difference in pronunciation of each of these words according to its function.

a. present (noun)
   present (adjective)
   present (verb)
b. desert (noun)
   desert (verb)
c. produce (noun)
   produce (verb)
d. conduct (noun)
   conduct (verb)
e. object (noun)
   object (verb)
f. absent (adjective)
   absent (verb)
g. protest (noun)
   protest (verb)
h. frequent (adjective)
   frequent (verb)
i. transfer (noun)
   transfer (verb)

j. subject (noun)
   subject (verb)

Repeat these words after the teacher. Take care to use extra breath force for the part of the word that the teacher stresses or uses more energy on.

Activity 3

Now fill in the blanks in the following sentences with the word in brackets (from the list above) and say whether it has been used as a noun/adjective or verb.

a. She promised to be .... at the meeting. (present)
b. They crossed the .... on camels. (desert)
c. She was awarded a prize for good .... (conduct)
d. They are planning to .... him to their office in Mumbai. (transfer)
e. Owing to failure of the monsoon agricultural .... is going to be very low. (produce)
f. Why did he decide to .... his battalion. (desert)
g. We have discussed the .... in great detail. (subject)
h. They asked him to .... his proposal to the committee. (present)
i. The residents .... to the cutting down of trees along the road. (object)
j. There is a .... shuttle service to the airport from several parts of the city. (frequent)

To the teacher: For higher classes the word in brackets could be removed and the instructions changed accordingly.

Activity 4

Listen to the information on population size and as you listen look at the following words and the context in which they occur. Then match each word on the left with its meaning on the right.

a. alarming	rise in the number of something	*i*
b. population	to show that something is likely or possible	*g*
c. slowed down	the limits between which something varies	*h*
d. current	causing worry and fear	*a*
e. trends	think or believe that something will happen	*k*
f. percentage	become smaller in number	*j*
g. indicate	a continuous fall in the number	*l*
h. range	the total number of people who live in a particular area, city or country	*b*
i. increase	reduced	*c*

j. decrease — a general direction in which a situation is developing *e*
k. expected — of the present time *d*
l. decline — the number of something expressed as if it is a part of a total of one hundred *f*

Activity 5 (Groups of 6)

Which word in the passage you have listened to is related to the word 'population'? (The word is an adjective.)

Look at the following words and think of words that are related to each of them. For example, the word *politics* has the following words that are related: *politician, political, politicise, polity*.

a. democracy (noun) *democratic, democrat, democratisation*
b. telegraph (noun) *telegraphy, telegraphic*
c. photograph (noun) *photography, photographic*
d. academy (noun) *academic, academician*
e. examine (verb) *examiner, examinee, examination*
f. indicate (verb) *indication, indicative*
g. expect (verb) *expectancy, expectation, expectant*
h. appear (verb) *appearance*
i. prefer (verb) *preference*
j. music (noun) *musical, musician*
k. commerce (noun) *commercial*
l. economy (noun) *economical, economist, economics*
m. admit (verb) *admission, admissible*
n. differ (verb) *difference*
o. beauty (noun) *beautify, beautiful*
p. electric (adj.) *electrical, electricity, electrician, electrify*
q. attractive (adj.) *attract, attraction*
r. government (noun) *govern, governor*
s. revise (verb) *revision*
t. divide (verb) *division, divisive*

To the teacher: Only those words that are suitable for the level of a particular class should be selected. Other words can be added to the list from the English textbook of the class concerned. The students could be asked to identify the part of speech of the related words in each case. They could look them up in the dictionary for usage. You can link this exercise to speaking by using the following activities.

ACTIVITY 6

Listen to the pronunciation of the related words above and repeat them after the teacher.

ACTIVITY 7 (GROUPS OF 6)

Look again at the chart you have filled in. Take turns to compare the percentage of population in 2000 according to age range with the percentage of population expected in 2050 in the same age group. You could use the following expressions to begin.

The percentage of population in the age range ....in 2050 is likely to/ expected to increase/decrease by ....%.

In 2000, the percentage of population in the age range of ....is higher/ lower than the percentage indicated/expected in 2050.

ACTIVITY 8 (GROUPS OF 6)

Discuss the following.

a. Will the slow down in population growth be beneficial to the country? What advantages will this have for India?
b. Will the decrease in percentage of population in the younger age groups give rise to any problems?

ACTIVITY 9

One member of each group could present the view of the group regarding the two questions above.

To the teacher: You will need to select those activities/portions of activities that are relevant to the level of your class. You can add to the activities given here.

CLASSES 9/10

How to demagnetise a screwdriver using a coil
(*English Reader IX*, First language English, Karnataka Textbook Society)

ACTIVITY 1

Listen to the instructions carefully and carry them out as you listen.

- Place the magnetised screwdriver blade inside a coil.

- Pass an alternating current through the coil.
- Slowly withdraw the coil to some distance while the current is flowing.
- When the screwdriver becomes demagnetised, switch off the current.
- Place the screwdriver in iron filings. If it does not attract the filings it has been demagnetised.

To the teacher: You can link this activity to speaking by using the following activity.

Activity 2

Each member of the group gives instructions to the rest of the group on how to demagnetise a screwdriver using a coil.

Activity 3 (Groups of 6)

Each member of the group then gives the other members instructions on how to make anything that they are good at making. It could be making tea, potato chips, a kite, a paper plane or other toys, flowers with paper, etc., and the others follow the instructions.

Unit 4

Classes 5/6

(*Gul Mohar Reader 4*, pp. 17–20)

Listen to the story 'The King of the Golden River'.

Raju was a poor fisherman. He lived on the banks of a stream that flowed into a big river. When the sunlight shone on the water, the stream looked like a thin, golden ribbon. So people called it the Golden River.

Early one morning, before the sun was in the sky, Raju took his net and walked over the cold sand to the water. A few stars were still shining in the sky.

Raju was hungry. 'I must catch plenty of fish this morning,' he said to himself. 'If I don't catch any fish, we shall not have much to eat today.'

For a long time, Raju pulled his net through the stream, but he did not catch any fish. The stars left the sky. The sun rose and it became hot. Raju wanted to go home, but just then he felt a tug.

Raju pulled the net to the bank and found a beautiful, golden fish inside. To his surprise, the fish spoke to him. 'Throw me back into the water,' it said. 'Please throw me back. If I lie in the hot sun, I'll die.'

Raju looked at the fish. It shone as brightly as the sun. It was certainly very beautiful. He felt sorry for the fish. He took it carefully out of the net and threw it back into the stream. Then, he went home.

That night, Raju's wife had only a little rice, which she made into a thin soup. The family sat round the small fire that burned outside the hut. Just then, an old man came slowly along the river path and stopped beside Raju and his family.

'May I rest here, please?' he asked. 'Tomorrow, I'm going to cross the river.'

'You are welcome,' said Raju. 'Sit by the fire and eat with us. I'm afraid we have only a little soup.'

The family had only one mat. Raju took it out and put it beside the fire. 'Sleep thee, Father, until it is light,' he said. 'In the morning, I'll take you across the river. If you try to cross the river by yourself, you may drown.'

Raju woke early the next morning. But the old man had already gone.

'How can he cross the river by himself?' Raju said to his wife. He ran along the river bank, but he could not find the old man. Then he took his boat and crossed the river, but no one on the other side had seen the old man.

That night, Raju's family ate only rice soup again.

The next morning, Raju took his net to the river again. He felt weak because his stomach was empty. At last, he felt a big fish fall into his net. He pulled it to the river bank. Inside was the beautiful, golden fish.

'Throw me back into the water. Please throw me back,' cried the fish again.

'But, if I throw you into the river, my family will have nothing to eat,' cried Raju.

'Please throw me back,' whispered the fish, in a voice that was now weak. 'If I lie in the hot sun, I'll die.' The fish tried to jump, but it was not strong enough.

Raju looked at the beautiful fish, and he felt sad. 'I can't allow such a beautiful thing to die,' he thought. And he threw the fish into the river.

That evening, Raju heard the sound of many drums and bells. He saw some men approaching his hut. They carried a big, red umbrella. Under the umbrella walked a man dressed in gold with a gold turban on his head. Behind him were drummers and musicians.

Raju waited for him and the others to pass. But they stopped in front of his hut.

'Raju, Raju,' the man called. 'I am the king of the Golden River. I was the old man, and you gave me food. I was the golden fish, and you saved my life twice. You were kind and helpful to me. Now, I want to help you in return. Please come and live in my house and look after my golden fish.'

So Raju and his family went to live in the king's golden house beside the river. The king's lakes were full of beautiful, golden fish. Raju gave them food and looked after them. He lived there happily with his family all the days of his life.

Classes 6/7/8

Activity 1

Listen carefully to a short talk and give it a title. (What is the talk about? Listen to the first few sentences to find out.)

The Earth takes 365 ¼ days, that is, one year to orbit the sun. Throughout the year, different parts of the world receive varying amounts of sunlight and these variations bring about the seasons. Owing to the Earth's axis—an imaginary line through its centre—which is tilted at an angle of 23.5 degrees, different parts of the planet are closer to the sun at different times of the year. For example, the Northern Hemisphere is closer to the sun from March to August and therefore has the spring and summer seasons during those months. In other words, the different hemispheres, or halves of the planet have different seasons at any given time in a year. Thus, in March, when the weather starts to warm up in the Northern Hemisphere, it cools down in the Southern Hemisphere.

In different regions, either changes in temperature or the amount of rainfall mark the different seasons. In most regions there are four seasons—spring, summer, autumn and winter. But in tropical zones, the difference in seasons is measured by the amount of rainfall rather than temperature. So the seasons are either wet or dry depending upon the period when it rains. When there is no rain, it is dry, that is immediately after the rainy season it remains cool and dry. Then just before the rainy season sets in again it becomes warm and humid.

In India we have roughly five seasons—spring, summer, the monsoon, autumn, winter. We have spring in February and March, summer from mid-March to mid-June, the rainy season or the monsoon from mid-June to October, and autumn in November and December. This is followed by winter from mid-December to mid-February. The period for these seasons varies slightly depending upon the direction—north, south, east or west—and so does the extent of the heat, the cold and the rain, that is the temperature and the amount of rainfall.

Activity 2

While you listen, write down the meanings of the following words. (Listen for the meanings in the talk.)
axis:
hemisphere:

Activity 3

Listen to the talk again and see how the following words are related to each other.

To the teacher: This may be put up on the blackboard.

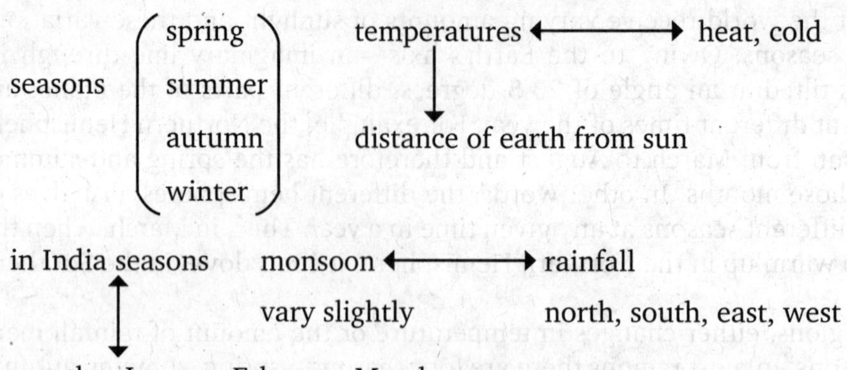

months: January, February, March, etc.

Each speaker then mentions two means by which the seasons are defined. (temperature, rainfall)

ACTIVITY 4 (GROUPS OF 6)

Match the words in column A with their meanings in column B.

A	*B*
axis	warm and damp
seasons	a position with one side or end higher than the other
tilted	the measurement in degrees how hot or cold a place or thing is
planet	any of the four main periods of the year—spring, summer, autumn, winter
hemisphere	an imaginary line through the centre of an object
temperature	one half of the earth, especially the half north or south of the equator
humid	the area between the two imaginary lines round the globe: the Tropic of Cancer in the north and the Tropic of Capricorn in the south, which is the hottest part of the earth.
tropical (zones)	a large round object in space that moves around a star (such as the sun) and receives light from it e.g. the Earth.

To the teacher: You can link the above activity to speaking, by using the following activity.

ACTIVITY 5

Listen carefully to the talk again, and as you listen fill in the following.

a. Different parts of the planet are closer to the sun at different times of the year because the Earth's ....
b. The Northern Hemisphere is .... and therefore has the ....
c. In March, when the weather starts to warm up in the ...., it cools down in the ....
d. ....in ....the difference in seasons is measured by the amount of .... rather than .... so the seasons are either .... or ....
e. In India the period for these seasons varies slightly depending upon the direction. .... and the ....also vary.

Activity 6 (Groups of 6)

Discuss what happens in spring or summer or the monsoon or autumn or winter. (Are there words in your language for the five seasons? For example, during the monsoon it rains very often and the sky is overcast on most days.) Use the following ideas to help you.

a. What is the weather like? (temperature, wet or dry, hot and/or humid, cold, freezing)
b. What happens when there is too much rain, heat, cold, etc.? (floods, dry, deaths)
c. What happens when there is too little rain, too little heat, etc.? (drought, crops affected)
d. What adjective/s would you use:
   i. for a winter that is extremely cold (e.g. severe, harsh, hard)?
   ii. for a winter when it is not very cold (e.g. mild)?
   iii. for a summer that is very hot (e.g. scorching, hot)?
   iv. for a monsoon when we get sufficient rain (e.g. good)?

Activity 7 (Groups of 6)

Tell the members of your group which season you like best and why. You could begin in any of the following ways.

I like .... best because ....

or

.... is the best season because ....

or

In my opinion ...., is the best season because ....

(The reasons could be those that relate to you as an individual or to a community, for example farmers, or general issues which concern society as a whole, for example, the environment.)

To the teacher: A globe or map could be used to show students the axis, hemisphere, Tropics of Cancer and Capricorn, the equator, etc., after they have listened to the passage.

Classes 9/10

Activity 1

Listen to a short talk on the CD. Listen for what it is about. Give the talk a title and write down the main idea in two sentences. While you listen, look at the following words. They will provide you with clues to what the talk is about.

Myanmar	pro-democracy struggle
military regime	inextricably involved
National League for Democracy	student revolt
house arrest	vowed
advocated	non-violence
despotic	prison
outraged	indomitable
struggle	ramping up
freedom	

It was in the year 1947 that General Aung San, one of the greatest freedom fighters of Myanmar was assassinated. He had led the freedom struggle against British colonialism. His daughter Aung San Suu Kyi was then only two years old.

At this point of time, Suu Kyi's mother was appointed Burmese ambassador to India. Suu Kyi went to school in New Delhi. It was here that she was greatly influenced by Mahatma Gandhi's ideals particularly the path of non-violence, which she was to follow in later years. Suu Kyi studied for a Bachelor's degree at the Lady Shri Ram College in New Delhi and then went to Oxford to continue her studies. After her studies at Oxford, Suu Kyi married a British tibetologist and settled down in England. She had two sons. In 1985, she registered for a PhD at the University of London. In 1988, she returned to her homeland, leaving her family behind. Her return coincided with the pro-democracy struggle against the military regime, in which she became inextricably involved.

It was then that she founded the National League for Democracy which comprised mainly students. She addressed massive gatherings with a view to making Myanmar a democratic country. The movement gathered momentum and spread rapidly throughout the country—so much so that the military government felt threatened. It was afraid it would lose its power.

The student revolt, the violence and bloodshed that followed led to the loss of hundreds of lives and a crushing defeat for the pro-democracy movement. A year later on July 20, 1989, Suu Kyi was placed under house arrest in Yangon. The military junta offered to release her on the condition that she should leave the country and never return. Suu Kyi refused to leave her country and vowed to fight for democracy but advocated the path of non-violence throughout. Though she was not accessible to the people, she continued to be a source of inspiration to them.

In 1990, the military generals, under immense international pressure decided to hold a democratic election. Suu Kyi and her National League for Democracy swept the polls winning 392 out of 485 seats in the Central Assembly of Parliament. But the military junta brushed aside the verdict and continued to rule. Suu Kyi continued to be confined to her house and refused to compromise with the harsh military regime. It was at this time that she won international acclaim. She won the Sakharov Peace Prize for freedom and the Nehru Peace Award in 1990 and the 1991 Nobel Peace Prize for freedom. Suu Kyi remained under house arrest for six years. The junta were, however, compelled to release her on July 11, 1995, for further fear of sanctions that Japan and the West might impose. Her release only strengthened her resolve to free the country from the clutches of the despotic military regime using non-violent means.

Since 1995, Suu Kyi has been in and out of prison several times. According to the latest news, she was to be released on May 27, 2009 but just a few days before her release, the military junta brought the charge of violation of house arrest against her on the grounds that she gave shelter to an uninvited American. It is possible that the trial would lead to her imprisonment for another five years. This has outraged the world and has led many countries in the West to say that they are considering ramping up sanctions against the military junta.

The charge against Suu Kyi is widely considered a pretext to keep her under detention ahead of the elections the military government has planned for next year.

Trial or no trial the indomitable Suu Kyi continues the struggle for the freedom of her people, and is a constant source of inspiration to them.

(Adapted from the English supplementary reader for class 10, Tamil Nadu Textbook Corporation, Chennai, 2004/2008, pp. 200–203.)

Activity 2

Look up the meanings of the words given above in the dictionary and listen again to them as used in context.

Activity 3

Given below are dates of some important happenings in Suu Kyi's life. Listen carefully to the talk and fill in the event(s) against each date.

1947	
1985	
1988	1. 2.
20 July, 1989	
1990	1. 2.
1991	
11 July, 1995	
22/23 May, 2009	
27 May, 2009	

To the teacher: More activities requiring students to listen for detail could be designed (for example, filling in the blanks and matching lists).

Activity 4

Can you say in which year Suu Kyi was born? (Listen carefully to the first few sentences for the answer.)

Activity 5

Look at the following questions and listen to the talk for the answers.

a. Where did Suu Kyi go to school, college and later university?
b. Which Indian leader was Suu Kyi's influenced by in her struggle for democracy?

Activity 6 (Groups of 6)

Discuss the difference between democracy and dictatorship. (Each member of a group could contribute at least one difference between the two.)

To the teacher: Some of the main differences are as follows.

Democracy	*Dictatorship*
1. government by many not by one	1. one-man rule (military or civilian)
2. government 'by the people, of the people, for the people'	2. government by a single dictator who has usurped power
3. government carried by the elected representatives	3. government not representative of the people
4. follows the principles of liberty equality, fraternity	4. government that does not allow freedom of speech or equality among men
5. government based on social justice (equality in the eyes of the law)	5. government that does not recognise equality before the law (justice dispensed according to the whims and fancies of the dictator who dictates the law)
6. government based on decentralisation of power	6. power is centralised in one man—the dictator

Activity 7 (Groups of 6)

Which form of government do you prefer—democracy or dictatorship? Give reasons. (Each member contributes at least one reason for their choice.) You could begin like this:
I think ... because ...
or I am of the opinion that ...because ...
or I am convinced that ...because ...
or There is no doubt that ...because ...
or It has been proved that ...because ...
The group notes down the reasons given by its members for their preference and one representative presents the points of view to the class.

Unit 5

Classes 4/5/6

Look at the following words and listen to them on CD.

bat mat
cat pat
fat rat
hat sat

To the teacher: You can pick out similar words from a lesson in the students' English reader.

Activity 1

Which two letters in each word have the same sounds? Write down the letter in each word that has a different sound. (/b/, /c/, /f/, etc.)

Activity 2 (Groups of 6)

In the words above, if you change the letter that has a different sound, you get a new word. For example, if 'b' in the word 'bat' is replaced with 'c' in the word 'cat' you get a new word. Notice that these words have 'at' in common. The only difference between one word and the other is the sound of the first letter, that is */b/* and */k/*. Now each group can pick one of the following words and write down as many words as they can with the same ending. First listen to the sounds in each of these words.

a. pin b. sun c. seat d. get e. hot f. can

A member of each group will write its list of words on the blackboard.

For the teacher:

bin	run	beat	bet	pot	ban
tin	fun	heat	let	cot	fan
fin	bun	neat	net	lot	pan
sin	gun	meat	set	got	ran
win	nun	treat	pet	rot	man
(din)	(pun)	(feat)	jet	not	van
(kin)	(shun)	cheat	yet	dot	(tan)
chin		wheat	wet	(jot)	van
thin					

Not all the students would know the words in brackets, particularly if they have English as a second language. You can add to the list of words the students write.

Activity 3 (Groups of 6)

Listen to each of the words from the lists you have prepared and write them down under the words below that they sound like. For example, the word 'din' would be written under the word 'pin'.

a. pin b. sun c. seat d. get e. hot f. can

To the teacher: Say the words in the lists at random, for example 'fun', 'not', 'cheat', 'wet', 'van', 'chin', and so on.

Activity 4 (Groups of 6)

Listen to the following words. They sound like the words in one of the six lists of words, but are spelt differently. For example, you hear the word 'son'. It sounds like the word 'sun' but is spelt differently.

a. feet b. debt c. what d. none

(*To the teacher*: Write the words on the blackboard and pronounce them again.)
What is the difference in the spelling of these when compared to the list of words they belong to.

For the teacher:

The word feet is spelt with 'ee' instead of 'ea'. Another example is 'sheet'. In the word 'debt', the letters 'eb' correspond to 'e' in the words under 'get'. The 'b' in the word is not pronounced. It is silent. In the word 'what', the letters 'ha' correspond to 'o' in the words under 'hot'. The letter 'h' is not pronounced. In the word 'none', the letters 'o' corresponds to the letter 'u' in the words under 'sun'. The letter 'e' is not pronounced.

Activity 4

Here are some more words. Under each word write down more words that have only one sound that is different. For example, for the word 'late', the letters 'ate' should be common to all the words under it, for example 'date', 'fate', 'rate' and 'mate'.

a. bat b. cast c. bow d. all e. light

For the teacher:

a. cat	b. fast	c. cow	d. ball	e. fight
fat	last	how	call	might
hat	mast	now	fall	might
mat	past	row	hall	right
rat	vast	vow	tall	sight
that	blast	wow	wall	tight
sat	(pun)	sow (n.) (female pig)		flight

Activity 5 (Groups of 6)

Can you think of words that have a different spelling but are pronounced with the same vowel sound in any of the words under a–e above. For example, under (b), the word 'caste' is spelt differently but sounds like 'cast', 'fast', etc.

For the teacher:

a. pl*ai*t (the same sound as the vowel in 'bat')
b. b*ou*gh (the same sound as the vowel in 'cow')
c. h*au*l, cr*aw*l, tr*aw*l (a search through a large amount of information) (the same vowel sound as the vowel in 'all')
d. *site, trite, mite, kite, height* (the same vowel sound as in 'fight')

Activity 6 (Groups of 6)

Listen to each of the following words and as you listen write down another word that sounds like each of them. For example, 'kind', 'find' and 'mind'.
(*To the teacher*: Write the words on the blackboard: call them out.)

a. caught	b. good	c. boat	d. phone	e. food
f. make	g. boil	h. hear	i. tour	j. turn

After you finish, ask your group leader to write your list of words on the board.

For the teacher:

a. bought	b. would	c. coat	d. tone	e. mood
taught	wood	note	bone	rude
fought	could			should
f. take	g. boil	h. dear/deer	i. poor	j. burn
lake	toil	fear	moor	learn
bake	soil	near		yearn
cake	foil	tear		fern
wake		rear		urn

Students would naturally give examples of words they know. Words that the teacher thinks are difficult for his/her students need not be cited as examples. If they are cited, then the meaning of those words would need to be explained in context.

Activity 7

Read aloud the examples that have been written under the words a–j.

To the teacher: Words that are mispronounced need to be corrected.

Activity 8 (Groups of 6)

Now look at all the words you have written so far. Pick out those consonant sounds that are different in these words. For example, in the words 'bat', 'cat', and 'fat', the letters 'b', 'c' and 'f' represent the three different consonant sounds /b/, /k/ and /f/.

For the teacher: The following consonant sounds occur in the words listed in Activity 2.

/b/	/k/
/f/	/h/
/m/	/p/
/r/	/s/
/t/	/w/
/v/	

Of the twenty-four consonant sounds in English only three have not occurred and these are /ŋ/ as in 'ring', /ð/ as in 'this', /z/ as in 'zoo' and /ʒ/ as in 'pleasure'. Students can be given examples of words in which these three sounds occur and told that there are twenty-four consonant sounds in English.

Similar activities can be designed to enable students to recognise and produce the vowel sounds.

Classes 6/7/8 (Sound and Spelling in Spoken English)

The relationship between the spelling and sound and the meaning of words can be effectively taught through listening. Dialogues and poems, recorded and played in class, or enacted in class are a useful means of exposing a student to spoken English. Listening followed by activities can effectively consolidate what the student has learnt by listening to the given piece.

Here is a poem that students in middle and high school would enjoy and benefit from.

Activity 1

Listen carefully to a poem about the English language.

The English language

Some words have different meanings,
and yet they're spelt the same.

A cricket is an insect,
to play it—it's a game.
On every hand, in every land,
it's thoroughly agreed,

the English language to explain,
is very hard indeed.

Some people say that you're a dear, yet dear is far from cheap.
A jumper is a thing you wear,
yet a jumper has to leap.
It's very clear, it's very queer,
and pray who is to blame
for different meanings to some words
pronounced and spelt the same?

A little journey is a trip,
a trip is when you fall.
It doesn't mean you have to dance
when'er you hold a ball.
Now here's a thing that puzzles me:
musicians of good taste
will very often form a band—
I've one around my waist!

You spin a top, go for a spin,
or spin a yarn maybe—
yet every spin's a different spin,
as you can plainly see.

Now here's a most peculiar thing,
'twas told me as a joke—
a dumb man wouldn't speak a word
yet seized a wheel and spoke.

A door may often be ajar,
but give the door a slam,
and then your nerves receive a jar—
and then there's jars of jam.
You've heard, of course, of traffic jams,
and jams you give your thumbs.
And adders, too, one is a snake,
the other adds up sums.

A policeman is a copper,
it's a nickname (impolite!)
yet a copper in the kitchen

is an article you light.
On every hand, in every land, it's thoroughly agreed
The English language to explain
is very hard indeed.
Harry Hamsley

Activity 2

While you listen pick out the lines that convey the poet's main message and write them down. (Listen to the ends of stanzas for your answer.)

Activity 3

Listen to the poem again and while you listen look at the following words and listen for their meanings.

cricket	ajar
dear	jam
jumper	adders
ball	copper
band	
spin	

Activity 4

Listen carefully for the two meanings of each of the words listed above in that order. You could make three columns as shown below. You could listen to one stanza at a time. The first word has been done for you as an example.

word	*meaning 1*	*meaning 2*
cricket	insect	a game
dear		

Activity 5 (Groups of 6)

Think of words that are spelt differently but pronounced alike. For example, the pairs of words *'sail'* and *'sale'*, and *'pain'* and *'pane'*, *'rain'* and *'reign'* have different spellings but are pronounced alike. You can use the dictionary for help.

Activity 6

A member of each group will put up its list of words and their meanings on the blackboard. Each group can then add to their list of words from those that the other groups have put up.

Activity 7

Look at the following words from the poem and listen to the pronunciation of the letter 'e' in the words 'cricket', 'insect', 'every' and 'copper'. What sounds does it represent?

For the teacher: The letter 'e' stands for different sounds. In the word 'cricket', it is pronounced like the vowel sound in 'bit', in the words 'insect' and 'every', it is pronounced like the vowel sound in 'set', in the word 'every', the second 'e' is not pronounced, and it is pronounced like the article 'a' in the word 'copper'.

Activity 8 (Groups of 6)

Look at the poem and listen carefully for words that have the letter 'a' and make a note of the different pronunciations it has in them. Make a note of all the words that have the letter 'a' and group them according to their pronunciations. For example, the pronunciation of the letter 'a' in the words 'fall' and 'ball' is the same.

Activity 9

A member of each group will put up the words on the blackboard. Listen to the CD once again and check the pronunciation of 'a' in the different words.

Activity 10

Listen for the pronunciation of the word 'queer' in stanza 2. Notice that the letter 'q' is pronounced */kw/*. Similarly, the letter 'x' stands for two sounds—*/ks/* as in 'excuse' and */gz/* as in 'example'. Can you give other examples of words spelt with 'q' and 'x'?

Activity 11 (Groups of 6)

You have identified four major types of examples of what makes spoken English difficult to learn. What are they? Discuss with the members of your group.

To the teacher: The activities have been so designed as to enable the student to do the following:

1. to listen for the message conveyed in the poem
2. to listen for detail, that is for the pronunciation of words and for the different meanings of the same word
3. to infer from the details the features that make spoken English difficult to learn
4. to use their existing knowledge to extend what they have learnt from listening to the poem, that is by adding more examples of words they know to the ones in the poem
5. to relate the written word to its pronunciation (what it sounds like).

Classes 9/10

Activity 1

Look at the poem below and listen to it carefully on the CD. Pay special attention to the pronunciation of the italicised words.

I take it you already know
Of *tough* and *bough* and *cough* and *dough*
Others may stumble, but not you
On *hiccough*, *thorough*, *lough* and *through*
Well done, And now you wish, perhaps
To learn of less familiar traps
Beware of *heard* a dreadful word
That looks like *beard* and sounds like *bird*
And *dead*—it's said like *bed*, not *bead*
For goodness sake, don't call it *deed*!
Watch out for *treat* and *great* and *threat*
They rhyme with *suite* and *straight* and *debt*
A *moth* is not a *moth* in *mother*
Nor *both* in *bother*, *broth* in *brother*
And *here* is not a match for *there*,
Nor *dear* and *fear* for *pear* and *bear*
And then there is *dose* and *rose* and *lose*
Just look them up—and *goose* and *choose*
And *cork* and *work* and *card* and *ward*

And *font* and *front* and *word* and *sword*
And *do* and *go*, then *thwart* and *cart*_
Come, come, I've already made a start
A dreadful language? Man alive,
I'd mastered it when I was five!

Author not known

Activity 2

Look at the italicised words in the first four lines. Have they got anything in common?. Now listen for the pronunciation of these words. Are they pronounced alike?

Activity 3

Now listen to lines 6–12. Pick out the words that are pronounced alike. Are they spelt alike? What is it that makes it difficult for us to know the correct pronunciation of these words? (Hint: Look at the words 'heard', 'beard' and 'bird'.)

Activity 4

Listen to the rest of the poem. While you listen, make a note of the words that you have been pronouncing differently. Correct your pronunciation by repeating them after the teacher on tape.

Activity 5

Can you say why you pronounced them as you did? Do you think your incorrect pronunciation is owing to any one or more of the reasons given below? Tick the reasons that apply to you.

a. They are spelt like other words you know the pronunciation of.
b. They are words you have never heard before.
c. They have consonant sounds that you cannot distinguish between, but the letter used in both is the same.
d. You were aware of the problem that pronouncing words as they are spelt can lead to incorrect pronunciation of those words.
e. Some other reason. (Give it.)

ACTIVITY 6 (GROUPS OF 6)

Write down pairs of words (other than the ones in the poem) that are spelt alike but pronounced differently, for example, 'heard' and 'beard', 'bough' and 'cough'. Write them on the board and pronounce them.

ACTIVITY 7 (GROUPS OF 6)

Now write down pairs of words other than the ones in the poem that are spelt differently but pronounced alike (for example, 'heard'/'bird' and 'sweet'/'suite').

ACTIVITY 8

Pick out words in the poem in which there is at least one silent letter, for example 'straight' ('gh' is silent).

ACTIVITY 9

In addition to the words from the poem, list as many words as you can with a silent letter/s.

ACTIVITY 10 (HOME ASSIGNMENT)

Write a similar short poem about the mismatch between spelling and sound.

CLASSES 9/10

ACTIVITY 1

Listen to the following dialogue. While you listen, look at the meaning of the words/ expressions on the blackboard. Then listen to the conversation again and underline those words that you hear as more prominent than the others in an utterance.

A: Where are you off to in such a great hurry?

B: I've to catch the three o'clock flight to Kolkata, and it's already eleven.

A: Don't panic. There's plenty of time.

B: No, there isn't. I have to go home, pack my bag, send for a taxi and pick up the other members of the team on the way to the airport.

A: D'you need any help?

B: No, thanks. I think I can manage (pause). If you'll excuse me, I really must be going.

A: Sure. I mustn't keep you any longer. Bye. Good luck.

B: Bye, and thanks.

For the teacher:
Gloss the following expressions:
off to
don't panic
pick up
can manage
keep you

Activity 2

Listen to the dialogue again and listen for that part of words that sound more prominent than the other parts. For example, the word 'where' is prominent in A's first utterance. Since it has only one vowel, it has only one syllable, which is stressed or heard as prominent. The word 'already' in B's first utterance is prominent. It has three parts, that is three vowels and therefore three syllables *al+rea+dy*. Of these three syllables, the second one, *rea*, is heard as more prominent than the other two. This syllable is stressed and has a vertical stroke above and in front of it. English words that have more than one syllable receive the stress on one of the syllables. The stress in English words has to be learnt.

To the teacher: If your students have not been introduced to features of pronunciation, such as the consonants and vowels, word stress, stress and rhythm in connected speech in English, and features that contribute to it e.g. contracted forms and weak forms, use the dialogue given above (Appendix 3). For sound and spelling in English, refer to the poem 'I take it … I was five!' and the activities that follow it (Appendix 5).

Examples of contracted forms in the dialogue: I've, isn't, don't, there's, won't mustn't

Examples of weak forms: a, to, the, and, there's, there, for, of, d'you (do), can

Consonant sounds: Point out important distinctions problematic sounds.
Vowel sounds: Almost all the vowels occur in the dialogue. The students can be asked to pick out those vowels in words that they have difficulty in recognising/producing/distinguishing between (any one, two or all of these).

where, are, good, of, in, such, great, catch, three
flight, already, don't, really, sure, you'll

To ensure that they can recognise and produce all these feature of spoken English, the students can be asked to enact the dialogue.

Activity 3

Of the prominent words in an utterance one is heard as the most prominent because the pitch of the speaker's voice changes on that word. For example, in A's first utterance the words 'off' and 'hurry' sound more prominent than the words 'where' and 'great' because the speaker's voice changes from high to low. Listen to the first utterance again. Then pick out the most prominent word/s in each utterance.

To the teacher:

Draw the student's attention to the different tones used in the dialogue—the falling for matter-of-fact statements/questions (Wh), the rising for continuity, listing activities or items, (for example, I have to go home, pack my bag, send for a taxi ... team ...), politeness (for example, No, thanks. I think I can manage), reassuring, friendly tone (for example, Don't panic. There's plenty of time, 'Yes' or 'No' questions (for example, D'you need any help?). Ask them to say what tone is used on each of the words that they have underlined as the most prominent. They would need to listen to the conversation several times in order to recognise the stressed syllables in words, the most prominent word in an utterance and the tone used on it.

Activities 4 and 5 are not compulsory and depend entirely upon the students' level of proficiency in English. They are more advanced and should be attempted by those students who have the ability.

Part 2

Appendix 6: Notes for the Teacher

Prompting to develop fluency

Visual Prompting

A variety of visuals can be used to help students to speak fluently. The effectiveness of a visual depends largely upon the kinds of activities the teacher designs to maximise interaction in the classroom. Most visuals can be used for more than one level by designing activities that have different difficulty levels.

A sample set of visual prompts and some group activities based on them and designed for different levels are given below.

- Students will look at the first picture and discuss the following with the other members of their group.
  a. What are the two white oval-shaped objects?
  b. Can you tell what the two creatures with the black and white stripes are?
  c. Does anything in the picture help you find out what they are?
- After all the groups have discussed the questions above, ask a member of each group to describe to the class what his/her group saw in the picture.
- Each group will next look carefully at the second picture and discuss the following.

a. Where are the two men? (in a forest)
b. What are they doing? (bending down to look at something)
c. What are they looking at? (a snake)
d. Are they afraid of what they are looking at? (no, seem fascinated)
e. Do you know what species of snake it is? (a cobra)
f. What helps you identify the species? (the hood and the mark on it)

- After all the groups have discussed the questions above, ask a member of each group to describe the picture to the class in four or five sentences.
- Students will tell the others in their group the names of poisonous snakes they know. The names of different types of poisonous snakes could be called out by each group and put up on the blackboard.
- 'All snakes are poisonous and very harmful and should be killed.' Each group can discuss the statement and decide whether they agree or disagree with it. They must give at least two reasons in support of their argument.

The visuals the teacher selects need not necessarily be taken from sources other than the textbook. Textbooks generally have pictures (particularly those for primary and middle school), which can be fruitfully used to motivate students to speak. In addition to pictures, visual prompts also comprise texts, statements, idioms/proverbs such as, which are general and those that relate to the passages/stories in the textbook.

Besides motivating students to speak, visual prompting helps them develop fluency and gain confidence. In order to achieve this, the teacher need not pay too much attention to accuracy but should encourage students to voice their instinctive responses/reactions to a picture or a piece of writing. Encouraging students to ask each other questions about the prompt, for example, would be an effective way of doing this.

Given below are some more examples of visual prompts from textbooks used in different states and notes on how they could be used in the classroom to promote speaking skills.

a. Look at the following pictures.

a cat

a bat

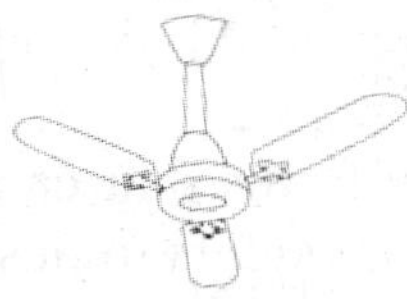

a fan

a cap

a man

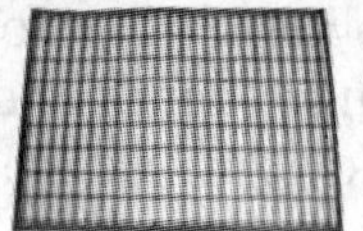
a mat

a bag

Any of the sets of pictures could be used to encourage students to take turns to ask questions and give answers. Question forms and responses that can be used include:

What's this?
What are these?
No, it isn't. It's a ….
No, they aren't. They are….
Is this/Are these…?
Yes….
What colour is …?
It is ….

These pictures could also be used for Class 5 when English is a second language as, for example, in Karnataka.

b. Look at the picture below.

The teacher could put the picture up on the wall and ask students to tell their classmates what they see in it. Visuals of this kind can help to prepare the students for the lesson. Those students who find it difficult to describe the picture on their own could be asked a number of simple questions by the teacher. The answers can be put up on the blackboard, leading to a description of a village based only on what students can see in the picture. Note that there are a number of things that the student cannot see at all or cannot see clearly in the picture, for example, the rice in the bags, the bags in the small boat, the fishermen and the flowers on the trees. A clearer coloured picture of a village would generate more spoken language.

Question forms that can be used to help the students to describe the picture include the following:

What is/are ...?
How many...?
Where is/are...?

c. Look at the pictures below.

Students could be asked to pick three games they like and three games they dislike playing. They can then tell the class the reasons for their likes and dislikes. The functions in this activity include expressing likes and dislikes and agreeing and disagreeing with others point of view. Students will learn to use the following expressions to express likes and dislikes:

I like .... and .... because ....

Of these three, I like .... because ....
My favourite game is ....because ....
The game I like most is .... because ....
I dislike ....most because ....

Students will learn to use the following expressions to express agreement and disagreement:

I agree with you that .... is a wonderful game.
Yes, you're right. We get a lot of fresh air when we play ....
I disagree with you. Indoor games are not boring. They are great fun.

Indoor games are good for rainy days.
But I like indoor games.
You may be right but ....

This picture could be used by students of Class 5 to talk about their favourite game and describe how it is played using the following frame.

- number of players
- positions of the players
- rules of the game (how points/runs/goals are scored, etc.)
- who is the winner

d. Look at the picture below.

The two pictures above could be used to teach students how to describe places and objects and to make comparisons in speech. The following activities could be used to do this.

Students could be divided into groups of six and each member asked to describe two things he or she sees in each of the pictures. The description of the members of each group can be put up on the blackboard.

The groups then compare the two pictures. They use antonyms to highlight the differences in the two pictures. Some of the antonyms that may be used are: 'tidy'/'untidy', 'empty'/'full', 'clean'/'dirty', 'even'/'uneven', 'straight'/'crooked' and 'light'/'dark'.

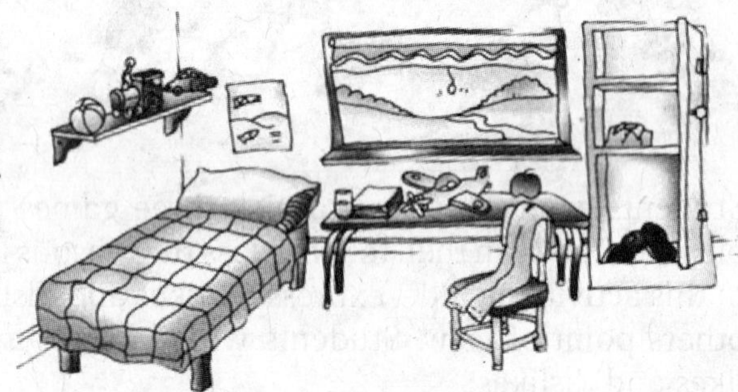

This visual input can also be used to teach students how to use colour words and comparatives to make comparisons. Comparatives they could use include:

tidier than
lower than
higher than
cleaner than
lighter than
darker than
straighter than
neater than
more cluttered than
less cluttered than

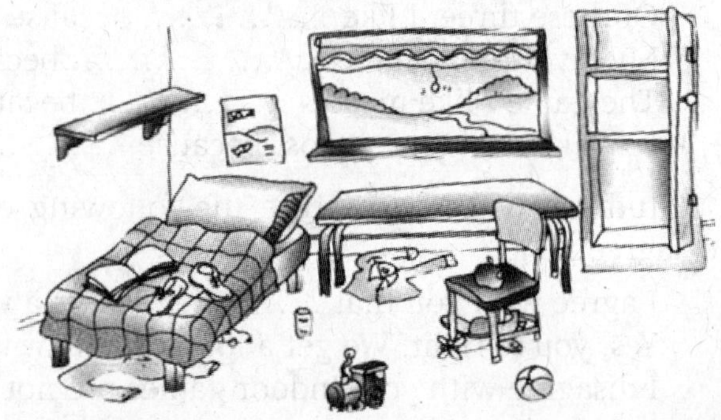

The comparative expressions used by each group to compare the two pictures could be put up on the blackboard. Each group could add to their list of adjectives and comparatives and talk about the two pictures to the class.

e. Look at the picture below.

Students can be shown the picture and asked to describe what the people and animals in it are doing. Verbs in the present continuous tense like 'play', 'swing', 'climb', 'sit', 'chat', 'feed', 'wait', 'rest' and nouns like 'boy/s', 'girl/s', 'child/children', 'man/men', 'bird/s', 'fruit', 'tree/s', 'trunk' and 'cattle/cow/s' can be provided as clues.

This activity can be linked to another one that helps the student use the present simple tense by dividing the students into groups and making each student tell their group what he or she likes to do during the interval in school. This will help them learn the use of the structure 'like' + *to* infinitive, as in: *I like + to swim*. Listed below are some of the phrases that may be used by students:

- to chat with my friends
- to eat my lunch
- to play games/football/cricket/badminton/tennis, etc.
- to climb trees
- to read a story book

Students can also be asked to talk about their hobbies. The following are some possible answers:

I like swimming.
I like reading.
I like playing (games).
I like travelling/sightseeing.

The input can also be used to teach students how to talk about preferences. Students could be asked to tell the members of their group which game or hobby they prefer to another and why. Help them with a list of outdoor and indoor games, for example cricket, football, basketball, badminton, chess, scrabble, ludo, snakes and ladders, and carrom. The following frame may be given to the students.

I prefer .... to .... because ....

f. Look at the pictures below.

These pictures can be used to make students tell a story. (Additional pictures showing the cap seller collecting his caps, putting them together and walking away with the bundle of caps would help students to tell the whole story.)

You can design a group activity based on the pictures in the following way.

- One student in a group could talk about one picture and the next member of the group could continue the story by building on what the previous member said. The last member in the group will complete the story. Students would tend to talk about the pictures in the present continuous tense, for example: 'A man is sleeping under a tree', 'A bundle is lying next to/near him', 'Many monkeys are sitting on the tree', 'They are wearing caps', 'The man is throwing a cap at the monkeys' and 'The monkeys are taking off their caps and throwing them down'.
- One student in each group could tell the class what the members of his group said about each picture. The sentences could be put on the blackboard.
- Each group tells the story with the help of the sentences on the board. (Give a hint to the students about the use of the simple past and past continuous tenses to narrate stories by putting the first few sentences on the blackboard and underlining the verb forms.) If you think the students need more help, you can write the story on the board with blanks for the correct form of the verbs in brackets.

A man *was sleeping* under a tree. He *was tired*. He was *carrying* a bundle. He *kept* it near him. When he .... (get/wake) up his bundle .... (to be) missing/not there. He .... (look) for it everywhere. It .... (be) nowhere. Then he .... (look) up and .... (see) many monkeys on the trees. They .... (be) wearing caps. He .... (do not) know what to do. Then he .... (think) of a plan. He .... (take) off his cap and .... (throw) it at the monkeys. The monkeys also .... (remove) the caps from their heads and .... (throw) them at him. The man .... (pick up) all his caps and .... (go) away.

Pictures in the English readers for classes 7, 8, 9 and 10 are very few. Visual prompts that can be used to get students to speak would, therefore, comprise quotations, statements, comments or proverbs from the lessons. Some sample texts are given below.

g.

MY STRUGGLE FOR AN EDUCATION

Booker T. Washington

1. One day, while at work in the coal mine, I happened to overhear two miners talking about a great school for coloured people somewhere in Virginia. This was the first time that I had ever heard about any kind of school or college that was more pretentious than the little coloured school in our town.
2. As they went on describing the school, it seemed to me that it must be the greatest place on earth. Not even heaven presented more attractions for me at that time than did the Hampton Normal and Agricultural Institute in Virginia, about which these men were talking. I resolved at once to go to that school, although I had no idea where it was, or how many miles away, or how I was going to reach it. I was on fire constantly with one ambition, and that was to go to Hampton. This thought was with me day and night.
3. In the fall of 1872, I determined to make an effort to get there. My mother was troubled with a great fear that I was starting out on a "wild-goose chase". At any rate, I got only a half-hearted consent that I might start. I had very little money with which to buy clothes and pay my travelling expenses. My brother John helped me all that he could; but, of course, that was not a great deal.
4. Finally the great day came, and I started for Hampton. I had only a small cheap satchel that contained a few articles of clothing I could get. My mother at the time was rather weak and broken in health. I hardly expected to see her again, and thus our parting was all the more sad. She, however, was very brave through it all.
5. The distance from Malden to Hampton is about five hundred miles. By walking, begging rides both in wagons and in the cars, in some way, after a number of days, I reached the city of Richmond, Virginia, about eighty two miles from Hampton. When I reached there, tired, hungry and dirty, it was late in the night.
6. Had never been in a large city, and this rather added to my misery. When I reached Richmond, I was completely out of money. I had not a single acquaintance in the place; and, being unused to city ways, I did not know where to go. I asked at several places for lodging, but they all wanted money, and that was what I did not have. Knowing nothing better to do, I walked the streets.
7. I must have walked the streets till after midnight. At last I became so exhausted that I could walk no longer. I was tired, I was hungry, U was everything but

discouraged. Just about the time I reached extreme physical exhaustion, I came upon a portion of a street where the board sidewalk was considerably elevated. I waited for a few minutes till I was sure that no passers-by could see me, and then crept under the sidewalk and lay for the night on the ground, with my satchel of clothing for a pillow. Nearly all night I could hear the tramp of feet over my head.

8. The next morning I found myself somewhat refreshed, but I was extremely hungry. As soon as it became light enough for me to see my surroundings, I noticed that I was near a large ship. It seemed to be unloading a cargo of pig iron. I went at once to the vessel and asked the captain to permit me to help unload the vessel in order to get money for food. The captain, a white man, who seemed to be kind hearted, consented. I worked long enough to earn money for my breakfast and it seems to me, as I remember it now, to have been about the best breakfast that I have ever eaten.
9. My worked pleased the captain so well that I could continue working for a small amount per day. This I was very glad to do. I continued working on this vessel for a number of days. After buying food with my small wages there was not much left to pay my way to Hampton. In order to economize in every way possible, I continued to sleep under the sidewalk.
10. When I had saved enough money with which to reach Hampton, I thanked the captain of the vessel for his kindness, and started again. Without any unusual occurrence I reached Hampton, with a surplus of exactly fifty cents with which to begin my education. The first sight of the large, three-storey, brick school building seemed to have rewarded me for all that I had undergone in order to reach that place. The sight of it seemed to give me new life.
11. As soon as possible after reaching the grounds of the Hampton Institute, I presented myself to the head teacher for assignment to a class. Having been so long without proper food, a bath, and a change of clothing, I did not, of course, make a very favourable impression upon her. I could see at once that there were doubts in her mind about the wisdom of admitting me as a student. For some time she did not refuse to admit me, neither did she decide in my favor. I continued to linger about her, and to impress her in all the ways I could with my worthiness. In the meantime I saw her admitting other students, and that added greatly to my discomfort. I felt, deep down in my heart, that I could do as well as they, if only I could get a chance to show what was in me.
12. After some hours had passed the head teacher said to me, “The adjoining recitation room needs sweeping. Take the broom and sweep it.”
13. It occurred to me at once that here was my chance. Never did I receive an order with more delight.
14. I swept the recitation room three times. Then I got a dusting cloth, and I dusted it four times. All the wood work around the walls, every bench, table and desk, I went over four times with my dusting cloth. Besides, every piece of furniture

had been moved and every closet and corner in the room had been thoroughly cleaned. I had the feeling that in a large measure my future depended upon the impression I made upon the teacher in the cleaning of that room. When I was through I reported to the head teacher. She was a 'Yankee' woman who know just where to look for dirt. She went into the room and inspected the floor and closets; then she took her handkerchief and rubbed it about the woodwork about the walls, and over the tables and benches. When she was unable to find one bit of dirt on the floor, or a particle of dust on any of the furniture, she quietly remarked, "I guess you will do to enter this institution."

15. I was one of the happiest souls on earth. The sweeping of that floor was my college examination. I have passed several examinations since then, but I have always felt that this was the best one I ever passed....

(*English Reader*, Class 8, Andhra Pradesh, pp. 35–37)

Some group activities you can design using the text above are as follows.

- Each group will discuss why they think the headteacher found the boy fit to be admitted. In other words, what was the teacher testing?
- Students will discuss the qualities that the headteacher was looking for to admit the child to the institute. Each group could tell the other groups the qualities they think were required, giving examples from the story of those that the child possessed.
- Each group could think of an idiom that would be a suitable description of the story in 'My Struggle for an Education' and put it up on the blackboard.
- Students will tell the others in their group about an incident in their life when they worked hard and achieved what they wanted. This will help students practise the use of past tense forms.
- 'Every citizen has the right to education'. The members of each group will give at least three arguments in favour of the above statement with reference to India and three problems that make it difficult to bring this about.

h.

STAMPS

Yellow and crinkly books are a bibliophile's pride.
What about a philatelist?

A stamp is to many people, just a slip of paper that takes a letter from one town or country to another. They are unable to understand why we stamp collectors find so much pleasure in collecting them and how we find time to indulge in our hobby. To them it seems a waste of time, a waste of energy and a waste of money. But they do not realise that there are many who buy stamp, many who find the effort worthwhile and many who, if they did not spend their time collecting stamps, would spend it less profitably. We all seek something to do in our leisure time and what better occupation is there to keep us out of mischief than that of collecting stamps? An album, a packet of hinges, a new supply of stamps—and the time passes swiftly and pleasantly.

Stamp collecting has no limits and a collection never had an end; countries are always printing and issuing new stamps to celebrate coronations, great events, anniversaries and deaths. And the fascination of collecting is trying to obtain these stamps before one's rivals get them. Every sphere of stamp collecting has its fascination—receiving letters from distant countries and discovering old stamps in the leaves of dusty old books. Gazing at its little picture we are transported to the wilds of Congo, the homes of the Arabs, and the endless tracks of the Sahara desert. There is a history behind every stamp. The ancient Roman Empire, the Constitution of America, India's independence and the Allied victory, are all conveyed to our mind's eye by means of stamps. We see famous men—printers, writers, scientists, soldiers, politicians—and famous events. Stamps so small and minute contain knowledge that is vast and important.

(*English Reader*, Class 10, Tamil Nadu, pp. 141–143)

Students will group the advantages and disadvantages of having a hobby. For example:

	Advantage	*Disadvantage*
a.	Hobbies help you spend your leisure hours profitably.	Hobbies mean a waste of a lot of time that you could spend on your studies.
b.	Hobbies provide you with opportunities to learn much more than what you learn in the classroom.	Hobbies are a source of distraction. They do not add to the knowledge you acquire from your textbooks.

- Students can be asked to consolidate the points discussed and present the advantages/disadvantages of having a hobby to the class.
- Students will talk about their hobbies/favourite hobby with their group and say why they enjoy them (for example, a good pastime, enjoyable, gives good deal of knowledge/information, adds to what the teacher teaches in the classroom, excellent recreation, physical and mental exercise, a window to the world, keeps one up-to-date, gives practical experience and allows one to get to know more about other people). Students could begin by telling the group how they chose the hobby, how they got interested in it, when they find time for it, what they have learnt from it and what else they think they will learn from it in the future.
- Those students who have the same hobby could then form a team, pool their information and tell the class more about their favourite hobby.

AUDIO PROMPTING

Audio prompting is a useful device that can prove to be very rewarding. The input should act as a powerful motivator and encourage students to be accurate by starting with imitation (repetition of dialogues they listen to that leads to the acquisition of formulaic expressions in relation to context and their use when provided with other similar contexts). The teacher could use snippets of news regarding current social issues to start a discussion. Announcements could be used to make students aware of what they need to listen for, for example, the facts in a particular context, the words and sentences used (vocabulary and grammar) and the clarity of the announcements (speed, correct pronunciation and modulation of voice).

Follow-up activities should help students make announcements in the context of their class and school. For example, they can be given the facts/content to come up with announcements regarding change in school timings or the timetable, timings and venues for practice for school events, etc.

PART 2

APPENDIX 7: ANSWER KEY

Unit 6

SOCIAL AND ACADEMIC CONTEXTS

ACTIVITY 1

The groups may list the following social contexts:
a. at home and the neighbourhood—with relatives, friends, etc.
b. at school—with classmates, teachers, the principal, visitors (invitees), etc.
c. at get-togethers with friends, relatives, strangers, etc.

Other contexts may be added to the list.

ACTIVITY 2

The groups may list the following academic contexts:
a. classroom and interschool interaction, discussion, debates, etc.
b. talks, presentations, compering, vivas, etc.

Other contexts may be added to the list.

Identifying context-related language

Activity 1

a. This is a formal setting. The use of the word 'shunt' (which means to move a train from one track to another or to move somebody or something to a different place because they are not wanted) is inappropriate in terms of the relationship between the participants and the register.
b. 'It's all right' is an appropriate response to 'I'm sorry' only when the latter is used to apologise and not when it is used, as in this case, to express sympathy.
c. 'You're welcome' is grammatical but cannot function as a reply to 'Thank you' said in response to a compliment. The use of 'You're welcome' is appropriate when the speaker has done somebody a favour.
d. The use of the word 'concoction' is inappropriate. It has been confused with the word 'decoction'.
e. Here again the word 'illegible' is wrongly used in place of 'eligible'.
f. The use of 'knowing' is incorrect. The *-ing* form is not used in English with 'mental' verbs.
g. Ramesh's reply is impolite and, therefore, inappropriate in the context of a polite offer of help.
h. Kalyan's reply to Sheetal's polite 'Excuse me' is inappropriate because it is rude. Sheetal's reply to Kalyan's question is also inappropriate because it sounds casual. Kalyan's reply is abrupt and unhelpful.
i. The student's reply to the teacher's question is incorrect because the teacher asks the student about an act that should have been completed. The student uses the wrong tense of the verb 'read' to answer the question.
j. Jacob does not make his identity clear. 'I'm Jacob from the fourth floor,' is inadequate and therefore not understood by Nisha.
k. There is a breakdown of communication because the Englishman uses the word 'tin' instead of the word 'can'. So the pun made by his friend does not come across at all.

Activity 2

a. Socioculturally, grammatically or contextually inappropriate/lack of clarity can be seen in Mr Rao's second utterance in dialogue (b) and Sunil's second utterance in dialogue (c) are socioculturally inappropriate. Dialogue (f) is grammatically incorrect. Dialogues (g) and (h) are socioculturally inappropriate.
   - Examples of socioculturally inapropriate language can be seen in dialogues (b), (c), (g) and (h).
   - Examples of grammatical incorrectness can be seen in dialogues (f) and (i).

  - Examples of lack of clarity can be seen in dialogue (j).
  - Example of contextually inappropriate language can be seen in dialogue (a).

b. Hilarious effect because of the use of a word other than the word intended can be seen in dialogues (d) and (e).
c. Breakdown of communication because of the use of a wrong word can be seen in dialogue (k).

Activity 3

a. Mr Kapadia: Certainly. I'll do it (send them upstairs) straightaway.
b. Mr Rao: Thanks for your concern.
c. Sunil: You haven't worn it before, have you?
d. Sangeetha: decoction
e. Farhan: eligible
f. Mr Kumar: I did not know there was a meeting.
g. Ramesh: Thank you very much. At present I've got people to do the job. I'll certainly take you up on your offer in future if I don't have help.
h. Kalyan: What can I do for you?
   Sheetal: I was wondering whether you saw Gita anywhere.
   Kalyan: No, I'm afraid not. Her secretary may be able to help you.
i. Student: Yes. I read them during the vacation.
j. Jacob: I'm Jacob from Orient Consultancy Services.
k. We eat what we can, and can what we can't.

Activity 4

a. obliterate
b. resolve
c. influence
d. desisted
e. phraseology

Activity 5

a. i. command, formal, certain
   ii. request, formal, polite
   iii. emphatic request, friendly, polite
   iv. question (negotiating), friendly, polite, uncertain
   v. request, formal, polite
b. i. request, formal, polite

ii. command couched in the form of a question, formal, authoritarian
iii. command (statement), formal, impolite, authoritarian
iv. request (statement) (direct—use of request word 'please'), formal, friendly, polite

c. i. question, informal/formal, neutral
ii. question, formal, polite (possibly someone in authority)
iii. statement (indirect question), formal/informal, authoritarian
iv. statement (assertive), informal, unfriendly, persistent
v. request (indirect), formal/informal, patient, friendly

d. i. statement (assertive), formal, friendly certain
ii. statement (assertive), informal, friendly, certain
iii. question, informal, friendly, proposition (invitation)
iv. statement, informal/formal, friendly, warm, certain
v. question (request), formal, friendly, polite

Unit 7

Visual Prompting

Activity 1

i. The pictures of flowers or objects like kites, which have many different colours, would attract students in classes 2 and 3 and would prove useful in teaching them basic colours and enabling them to distinguish between one colour and another. These pictures of flowers could be used in class 4 to teach the names of the parts of flowers.
The objective/s of the prompt would be to teach the students:
– the names of different colours } classes 2/3
– the names of different common flowers } classes 2/3
– the names of the parts of flowers } class 4
– how to describe making something, for e.g. a kite } class 4/5
(More complex activities may be designed for the higher classes. Thus, the prompts could be used to teach students in classes 6/7 to give instructions, for example, on making kites.)
The following are some group activities the teacher could use to achieve the objectives:
The teacher can use the picture of flowers by making students to take turns to ask and answer questions such as the following:
– What colour is ...? (naming, class 2/3)
– What is it called? (describing, class 4)

- What does it look like? (describing, class 4)
- As follow-up activity, students can be asked to collect pictures of as many flowers/ other objects as they can and tell their group the following:
- what colour/s they are (naming, class 2/3)
- what they are called (naming, class 4)
- what they look like (describing, class 4)

Note: Students might not know the colours of some flowers/objects. The teacher would need to monitor them closely.

An extended activity on combining colours to form other colours could be designed for students of classes 4, 5 and 6. Students can be given the basic water/crayon colours (red, green, blue, yellow, white) and each of them asked to tell his/her group which colours can combine to form a new colour. The names of the two colours mixed and the resulting colour could be put up on the board by the students. For example, red mixed with yellow gives orange, blue mixed with red gives purple, blue mixed with yellow gives green.

They could experiment with combining other colours.

Note: It is not necessary for the teacher to go strictly by the levels mentioned against the activities and confine themselves to only those activities. If their class is capable of participating in all the activities, it should be allowed to do so.

ii. The picture of a rainbow could probably be used as a visual prompt for classes 4, 5, 6, 7 and 8. It could be an extension of the activities on colours mentioned above to teach teach students to talk about shapes—starting with the curved rainbow to other similar adjectives, like 'bent', 'twisted', 'wavy', 'curly' and 'zigzag'. Higher classes could form nouns from these.

The objectives of the prompt would be:
- to familiarise students with the names of colours
- to familiarise students with the words for shapes
- to teach the noun forms of the adjectives that describe the different shapes (e.g. 'bend' and 'twist')
- to enable students to describe how a rainbow is formed (classes 6/7)
- to enable students to use the dictionary for other words attached to the word 'rain' (for example, rainfall and rainforest) and share the meanings of those words with the group/class.

Some group activities the teacher could use to achieve the above objectives are listed below.
- Each group of students can look at a picture of the rainbow and identify the colours in the rainbow. Each group then tells the others (a) how many colours the rainbow has (b) what the colours are. *Note*: Students may agree/disagree with each other regarding the answers to these questions. The teacher could guide them.
- Each group of students can tell the others why they think it is called a rainbow. (clues: rain, sunlight).

- Each group can describe to the class the shape of the rainbow (clue: bow). Given pictures of objects with other shapes, each group could identify the different shapes (bent, curly, twisted, wavy, zigzag, etc.).
- Students of classes 9 and 10 can describe different objects of a given shape (for example, a curved road/path/blade, a twisted rope/key/metal/plait, a bent spoon/finger, wavy lines/hair, curly hair/tail and a zigzag line/pattern/path). *Note*: These adjectives are used with nouns, that is, each one must be followed by a noun.
- Students of classes 9 and 10 can use the dictionary to find the noun forms of the adjectives above.
- Each group (from classes 9/10) makes a list of words beginning with 'rain' and tells the class the meanings of those words. (Examples: raindrop, rain dance, rainfall, rainforest, rainproof, rainstorm, rainwater, rainwear)

iii. The pictures illustrating events in stories would be useful as visual prompts for students in classes 4, 5 and 6. Students at this level like to tell stories and also listen to stories. Pictures in a sequence would make it easier for them to say what a particular picture is about and later tell the whole story. Alternatively, the teacher could use comic strips that tell a story.
The objectives would be:
- to teach students how to describe events using the present continuous tense
- to enable students to tell a story, after they have described the events in the pictures, using the past tense

Group activities the teacher could use to achieve the above objectives are:
- A series of pictures forming a story can be given to each group. One or two members of each group can be asked describe one picture in the story.
- The members of the group can then take turns to tell the story using their description of the pictures to guide them.
- Students (of classes 5 and 6) could be asked to make a list of verbs they used in describing the pictures. (present/present continuous forms)
- They could then make a list of the same verbs/other verbs (past tense) they used to narrate the story and put them up on the blackboard
- Each group could be asked to answer some of the following questions orally.
  a. Why was the crow not able to drink the water in the jug?
  b. What did the thirsty crow do to get water to drink?
  c. Was the crow successful?
  d. What word would you use to describe the crow?
     (clever, wise, resourceful, etc.)

Note: Similar activities could be prepared based on the other two stories. The teacher could extend this activity and encourage students to tell a story they have read in their textbook or one that is from some other source.

iv. The visual prompt of bees on a honeycomb could be used for classes 5/6/7/8/9, depending upon the activities the teacher designs. For example:

- Students of classes 2, 3 and 4 can be asked to describe what they see in the picture. (bees—their colours, parts of the body, hive appearance)
- Students can be asked to discuss what bees give us, how they are useful and how they can be harmful.
- Students can be asked if they like honey and asked to give reasons for their answer.
- Students can be asked to say what animals and birds like cows, goats and hens give us.

  Note: Students should be encouraged to speak. A group representative or the teacher should write what they say on the blackboard.
- Students of classes 6, 7 and 8 can be asked to read up on bees and tell the class how bees make honey and why they need to do so.
- Students can be asked to discuss the question 'Do we get most of our honey from the wild?' (Most of the demand for honey in the world is met by beekeepers who breed bees to obtain honey. This is known as 'apiculture'.) They can be asked to think of other words ending in 'culture'.

v. See Appendix 6.

vi. See Unit 6.

The picture of felled trees can be used as a visual prompt in classes 9 and 10.

- Students can be asked to describe the picture. (present continuous, present perfect tense)
- The following topics can be given to them for discussion:

  Should trees be cut mercilessly?

  Trees have to be cut to widen roads and for development.

  Indiscriminate cutting of trees can ruin the environment and disturb ecological balance.

  Is development worthwhile at the cost of the environment?

Audio Prompting

Activity 2

Dialogue 1

a. The prompt is suitable for classes 9 and 10.

b. The main objective would be to teach students about the features of speech, such as hesitation, and their function in conversation (here they signal a negative response). Students could also be taught the other functions hesitations serve, for example 'er', 'mm', etc., could also mean indecision or pausing to think of an answer to a question. Here, they are part of negotiating.

c. Activities would include questions, to begin with, regarding the context, the relationship between A and B, the meaning of 'er' and 'mm' in this context. Role play exercises could be designed by constructing contexts and asking students to participate in and enact dialogues. Sample contexts are given below:

i. Your friend is very good at maths. You would like him to help you. Find out when he can spend some time with you. Ask him whether a particular time would suit him. If not, suggest an alternative.

ii. Your teacher would like you to rehearse a play you are going to stage on the annual day. You need to know when all the actors in the play will be available for rehearsals every day. You ask the actors in the play whether they will be available in the afternoons. One of the actors says he will not be free on Mondays. You suggest that you could have the rehearsals on all other days except Mondays. Everyone agrees.

iii. The teacher has asked you to put up some charts in the classroom. You ask a classmate if he/she can spare some time during the lunch interval. Your classmate says he/she will be busy doing an assignment. You suggest an alternative that he/she agrees to. You thank him/her.

Other similar contexts can be constructed for role play. The students could exchange roles.

Dialogue 2

a. This is a suitable prompt for classes 9/10.

b. The objectives of this activity include teaching the student the difference between informal greetings ('hi', 'hello', etc.) and formal greetings ('good morning','good afternoon', etc.). They can also be taught the use of expressions such as 'No wonder…' and 'You bet I have.'

c. Students could be asked to enact the dialogue and exchange roles. Constructing similar contexts for students will enable them to practise informal interaction with friends or classmates. For example:

You go away to spend your vacation with your uncle. Your friends in your neighbourhood stay at home throughout the vacation. You return a few days before your school reopens, and your friend next door pays you a surprise visit. Your friend is surprised and very happy to see you and asks you where you went during the vacation. You greet him/her and say that you spent your vacation with your uncle. Your friend says he/she is not at all surprised that you are looking so well. You say you feel quite fit. Your friend says you must have enjoyed yourself. You say that you certainly did.

Students may be asked to write the dialogue and then enact it.

Dialogues 3 and 4

a. These prompts are suitable for classes 7, 8, 9 and 10.

b. Objectives include the following:

   i. teach different ways of making requests

ii. teach different ways of thanking someone for favours done
iii. teach different ways of responding to 'thank you' for favours done

c. Some sample group activities for dialogue 3 are given below. You could design similar activities for your students.
   i. Listen to the dialogue and then repeat after the teacher. Enact the dialogues in your group, exchanging roles.
   ii. Listen to dialogue 3 and answer the following questions.
      - Do the speakers know each other? Pick out those parts of the dialogue that support your answer.
      - Does A request or order B to take down the suitcase? What expression does A use to do so?
      - What does A say when B takes down the suitcase and what is B's response?
   iii. Write dialogues to suit the contexts below and enact them in your group to practise making requests and responding to them.
      - Your teacher asks you to fetch exercise books from the cupboard. You ask the teacher which ones you should fetch. She says that you should fetch the ones lying on the topmost shelf. You fetch the books and give them to her. She thanks you. You respond.

   Some of the expressions students could use to make polite requests are, 'Could you possibly…', 'Could you…please', 'Please…', 'D'you mind….—ing' 'Would you mind….—ing' and 'Would it be possible for you to …'.

   To respond positively to a request, students could use expressions such as 'Most certainly', 'Yes, of course', 'Certainly', etc.

   To respond negatively to a request, (as in dialogue 4), students could use expressions such as, 'I'm afraid not', 'I'm afraid he's/she's not …', and 'I'm sorry I can't/don't …'.

   (Note that students should be told that they must give reasons for their negative response.)

   To respond to a favour, students could use expressions like, 'Thanks a lot', 'Thank you so much', 'I really appreciate the trouble you took to…', 'It's very helpful of you to…', 'It's very kind of you to…', 'I'm really grateful for all your help' and 'I can't tell you how much I appreciate all the help…'

   In response to 'Thank you' students could use 'My pleasure', 'Don't mention it', 'Not at all' and 'Sure' (informal).

   The choice of expressions from the list above will depend on the context given to students.

      - Your friend asks you to do him/her a favour. You ask him/her what you can do for him/her. Your friend requests you to buy some notebooks for him/her from the stationer's next to your house. You agree and he/she thanks you. You respond to the thanks. The next day your friend tells you that he/she really appreciates the trouble you took to buy the notebooks and carry them to school.

- After they are done, help your students revise their dialogues.

iv. Enact in your group the dialogues you have written, exchanging roles.

d. Sample activities for dialogue 4 are given below.

i. Listen to the dialogue and then repeat after the teacher. Enact the dialogues in your group, exchanging roles.

ii. Listen to dialogue 4 and answer the following questions.

- Do the speakers know each other?
- Where do you think the conversation takes place?
- Is B able to grant A's request?
- What does B say?
- What is the expression A uses to request B for information?
- What is A's last request?
- Does B agree to it?

iii. Write dialogues to suit the contexts below and enact them in your group for practice.

- Your parents say they would like to meet the principal of your school. They request you to make an appointment for them. You approach the principal and inform him/her that your parents would like an appointment. You request the principal to let you know when (day and time) they can meet him/her. The principal says he/she can meet them on Friday, the 8th at 3 p.m. You thank the principal.
- You find it difficult to solve a sum in maths, so you want to ask your teacher for help. You approach one of your teachers in the staff room, and ask her politely where your maths teacher is. The teacher tells you your maths teacher has gone out on some urgent work. You ask her when he will be back. The teacher says that she is not sure, but probably by 4 o' clock. You request the teacher to convey a message, which she agrees to do. You thank the teacher and request her to tell the maths teacher that you came to see him for help. The teacher says she will. You thank the teacher.

Dialogues 5 and 9

a. These dialogues could be used as and audio prompts for classes 6 to 10.

b. The main objective of these prompts would be to teach students: how to introduce themselves and to introduce people to each other in formal and informal contexts.

c. Some sample activities for dialogues 5 and 9 are given below.

i. Listen to dialogues 5 and 9 and repeat after the teacher.

ii. Listen to dialogue 5 carefully and answer the following questions.

- Do A and B know each other? Give reasons for your answer.
- What words do they use to greet each other?

- Which one (A or B) is new to the school? Pick out three sentences in support of your answer.

iii. Enact the dialogue in groups of six. Replace the names in the dialogue with the names of the students in class. Exchange roles.

d. Construct contexts in which students themselves would need to introduce themselves. For example:
You are participating in an inter-school recitation competition. You meet a participant from another school. You greet her and tell her your name and ask for hers. She greets you and tells you her name. You tell her which school you are from and ask her which school she is from. You tell her which poem you are going to recite (name of the poem). She tells you which poem she is going to recite. You wish her the best of luck. She does the same.

For example:

- Kiran: Radha, I'd like you to meet my mother. Mama, this is my friend Radha.
  Mother: Pleased to meet you, Radha. Kiran talks a lot about you.
- Sharad: Mr Kumar, meet Dr Radha Dutt. She's the principal of our school.
  Mr Kumar: Pleased to meet you Dr Dutt. I'm from Navjyothi School.
  Radha Dutt: Pleased to meet you too. What can I do for you.
  Mr Kumar: May I invite you to be the chief guest on our annual day. Here's the invitation.
  Radha Dutt: Thank you. I'd love to be there.
  Mr Kumar: Thank you for accepting our invitation.

Dialogues 6 and 7

a. These dialogues would be suitable for classes 9 and 10. Making suggestions, and accepting or rejecting them are functions that require a fair amount of proficiency in English.

b. The objectives include teaching students:
   i. different ways of making suggestions.
   ii. different ways of agreeing/disagreeing with suggestions.

c. Some sample group activities are given below.
   i. Listen to dialogue 6 and repeat after the teacher.
   ii. Take turns to role play dialogues of both A and B.
   iii. Write dialogues to suit the contexts below and enact them in your group for practice.

- Your teacher tells you the school is organising a two-week excursion during the summer vacation. You are given the following place names to choose from: Ooty, Annamalai Wildlife Sanctuary, Ranthambore Tiger Reserve, Matheran, Kanyakumari, Darjeeling and Sikkim, the Ajanta Ellora caves and Kulu Manali. Each member suggests the place they would like to go to and other members of the group agree/disagree. They make their own suggestions. Your group finally agrees to suggest one of the places, and you tell the other groups where your group would like to go. The other groups agree/disagree with you and give reasons. They suggest other places and give reasons for their choice. Your teacher finally takes a decision after listening to all the groups.

- You would like to take part in a recitation competition. You meet your teacher. You suggest a couple of poems. Your teacher suggests alternatives and gives reasons (for example, the poems you have chosen are too long/difficult or there are too many big words in them). You agree that one of the poems your teacher suggests would be good/suitable for recitation. You thank your teacher for helping you to select the poem.

Here are some expressions that your students could use to make suggestions:

Why don't you...
I propose I/we....
I suggest you/we...
How about reciting...
You might try reciting ...

Unit 8

Use of functions in social contexts

Activity 1

Dialogue 1

a. The relationship between the participants is formal.

b. The conversation could take place at any public place—bus station, railway station, bank etc. The speakers do not know each other at all.

c. The functions that the speakers perform include drawing someone's attention, enquiring, thanking and responding to thanks.

d. 'Excuse me' (to draw attention), 'have you got...' (to enquire), 'thank you' (to thank) and 'you're welcome' (to respond to thanks) are the expressions used to perform the functions.

e. Yes.

Dialogue 2

a. The relationship between the participants is formal but friendly.

b. The conversation could take place at any public place or office.

c. The functions that the speakers perform include greeting, enquiring, responding to enquiries, requesting and responding to requests, proposing and responding to proposals, agreeing unwillingly, thanking and parting.

d. 'Hello…', 'how are…?', 'I'm quite well, thank you…', 'and you…?', 'oh, I'm …', 'could you …', 'I'm afraid …', 'may be …', 'yes. Perhaps.', 'thank you…' and 'bye' are the expressions used to perform the functions.

e. Yes.

Dialogue 3

a. The relationship between the participants is formal but friendly.

b. The conversation could take place at a party or at somebody's house.

c. The functions that the speakers perform include offering and responding to offers, enquiring and responding to enquiries and thanking and responding to thanks.

d. 'Would you……', 'yes, please', 'thank you…' (thanking) 'pleasure' are the expressions used to perform the functions.

e. Yes.

Dialogue 4

a. The relationship between the participants is extremely formal. A and B are strangers.

b. The conversation could take place at a public place like a bus-stop or on the road.

c. The functions that the speakers perform include drawing attention, enquiring and responding to enquiries, apologising and responding to apologies.

d. 'Excuse me', 'could…please', 'how should…', 'I'm sorry…', 'Oh, that's all right', are the expressions used to perform the functions.

e. No. B's reply to A's polite enquiry is rude. It violates the norms of politeness.

Dialogue 5

a. The relationship between the participants is friendly. They could be friends or colleagues.

b. The conversation could take place at the workplace, at the home of one of the participants or at a public place.

c. The functions that the speakers perform include apologising and responding to apologies, giving reasons and responding to them (sympathising), and enquiring and responding to enquiries.

d. 'I say, I'm…', 'I was so disappointed…', 'my brother…', 'that's…', 'how's he …' and 'better, thanks' are the expressions used to perform the functions.

e. Yes.

Dialogue 6

a. The relationship between the participants in very formal. They are colleagues.

b. The conversation takes place at the workplace.

c. The functions the speakers perform include apologising and responding to apologies, requesting, suggesting and thanking.

d. 'I would like...', 'It's a pity...', 'I wonder...', 'you could talk...' and 'thank you' are the expressions used to perform the functions.

e. Yes.

Dialogue 7

a. The relationship between the participants is formal.

b. The conversations takes place at a school.

c. The functions the speakers perform include requesting, ordering, assuring and ordering.

d. 'Please ensure...', 'we'll do...', 'if any...must be contacted immediately', are the expressions used to perform the functions.

e. Yes.

Dialogue 8

a. The relationship between the participants is informal. They could be friends, colleagues or classmates.

b. The conversation could take place at a school or college, a workplace or any public place.

c. The functions the speakers perform include enquiring, explaining, asking for reasons, stating or expressing necessity and giving reasons.

d. 'Where on earth...', 'went out...', 'why...', 'this is an...', 'we must meet...', 'yes, that's why...', are the expressions used to perform the functions.

e. Yes.

Dialogue 9

a. The relationship between the participants is informal but participant A is older.

b. The conversation could take place at A's office.

c. The functions the speakers perform include greeting, offering, requesting, agreeing, enquiring, wishing, thanking and parting.

d. 'Hello ...', 'what can ...?', 'could you...please', 'certainly, what for?', 'best of luck', 'Thank...' and 'bye, bye' are the expressions used to perform the functions.

e. Yes.

Dialogue 10

a. The relationship between the participants is informal. They are friends.

b. The conversation could take place at any public place.

c. The functions the speakers perform include confirming news and condoling.

d. 'I heard your …', 'I'm so …', 'I can't believe …', are the expressions used to perform the functions.
e. Yes.

Dialogue 11

a. The relationship between the participants is formal. They have never met each other before.
b. The conversation could take place at an award function.
c. The functions the speakers perform include greeting, introducing self, responding to greeting and introducing self, enquiring, informing, congratulating and thanking.
d. 'Good morning…', 'I'm Anandi from …' 'pleased to meet…', 'has your son…?' '…yours too?', '… my grandson's …', 'congratulations…' and 'thank you' are the expressions used to perform the functions.
e. Yes.

Dialogue 12

a. The relationship between the participants is informal. They are classmates.
b. They conversation could take place at a school or college.
c. The functions the speakers perform include enquiring and responding to enquiries, stating, informing, showing disapproval, responding, contradicting (disagreeing), suggesting, seeking advice, giving advice and accepting advice.
d. 'Where were you…', 'I went…', 'but it's…', 'it's okay', 'no, it isn't', what should I…', I'd apply', and 'all right' are the expressions used to perform the functions.
e. Yes.

Activity 3

Note: Given below are only some of the possible answers.

a. Greeting:
   Good morning/afternoon/evening (formal/formal-friendly)
   Hello/hi… (informal-friendly)
b. Interrupting/drawing someone's attention
   Excuse me
   Sorry, am I interrupting?
   Pardon the interruption…
   I'm sorry but …
   Sorry to interrupt you, but…
   Are you free for a minute?
   Have you got a minute?
c. Enquiring
   How are you…

How have you been…
What would you like?
Where were you…
When will they …
Why were (you)…
'Why are (they)…
Why have (they)…
How did you do…
'How many…
How much…
Which one of these would you like?

d. Requesting
Could you…
D'you mind…
Would you…
Please…
Could you do me a favour…
Would it be possible for you to help me…
I'd be grateful if you could…
May I request you to …

e. Thanking

f. Thank you so/very much… (formal)
Thanks so/very much… (not so formal)
Thanks a million. (not so formal)
Thank you for…

g. Apologising
I'm so/really sorry… (direct)
I must apologise for… (indirect)
I feel (so) bad to/about…
Please forgive me…

h. Accepting an apology
Oh, that's okay/fine.
Forget about it.
Never mind…
It doesn't matter…
Don't let it bother you…
I understand.

i. Making suggestions
I suggest we…
Why don't we/you…
I don't think it's …
May be you could…

Let's ...
Shall we ...
How about a... (a noun)?
How about ....—ing?
I think we need to ...
I propose we ...
Couldn't we ...?
We might try ...—ing

j. Responding to suggestions
That's a good idea...
That should help/be useful ...
We could give it a try/chance ...
That'd be so refreshing/relaxing/much fun.
Oh, no. That won't work.
Good idea.
That's not necessary.
There's no need for that.

k. Asking for advice
What should I/we do?
What can I do (to)...
D'you think it's right/proper/advisable/a good idea...
I don't know what to do?

l. Giving advice
They'd/you'd better ...
I/we/you should...
You ought to...
I'd advise you to...
If I were you I'd...
(I think) we'd/you'd better not ...

m. Expressing one's opinion
I think/feel/like/love/believe/dislike/hate/agree (with)/disagree (with)...
In my/our opinion...
I'm/we are of the opinion that...
From my/our point of view...
The way I see it...
In my view...
It seems to me that...

n. Expressing sympathy
I'm sorry (to hear...)
I'm really/terribly/very/extremely sorry...
I'm so sorry...
Oh! how terrible /awful/upsetting/annoying...

Oh! what a nuisance/disaster...
I can't tell you how sorry/upset I am...
I don't know what to say

Use of functions in academic contexts

Activity 5

The subskill the students would acquire include identifying and describing.

Activity 6

There are the mighty Himalayas in the north.
These mountains are very high.
They rise to the sky.
There is snow on the top of these mountains.
There are seas on three sides of our country.
There is the Bay of Bengal on the east, the Indian Ocean on the south and the Arabian Sea on the west.

Activity 7

The following words and phrases can be focussed on to teach vocabulary and pronunciation.

Mountains—high
Snow—beautiful
Directions—east, west, north, south
Seasons—summer, winter
Names of rivers—flow
Plains—grow (wheat, maize, etc.)

Note: Students generally imitate the teacher's pronunciation. Hence it is necessary for the teacher to pronounce all the words in the lesson correctly and clearly.

The following structures can be focussed on to teach grammar.

There is/are + noun or adjective + noun
This/that/these/those + noun + be verb
They + verb

Activity 8

Given below are some of the activities that may be devised.

a. Students could listen to the passage twice and mark the mountains and rivers on a physical map.
b. Students could take turns to identify the physical features of India in a map.
c. Students' attention could be drawn to the structures and vocabulary used by them by writing them the blackboard.
d. Each group of students could be given a picture and asked to identify familiar articles/objects/figures/animals in it. (They can use there is, there are, this is, (these are), these + noun + be + adj., etc.)
e. The picture each group has could then be put up on the blackboard and all the members of the other groups asked to identify at least two articles/objects/animals/plants etc. (This could be follow-up work.)

Activity 9

It would be possible to use this passage for classes 4 and 5 by extending identification to people, places, etc. and using demonstratives in addition to 'there is' and 'there are'.
For example:
That is it/him/her/them/the + noun.
Those are....
These are...

Pronouns could be used in places where nouns are used in adjacent sentences. Also, the use of present tense forms of verbs and adjectives could be taught.

The following sentences could be added to the previous list.

These mountains ...
They rise to the sky ...
There is snow on the top of them ...
They are covered with snow...
They (the mountains) look beautiful.
In summer... melts...
The big rivers... spring from ...
They flow down the hills, through the valleys, across the plains, into the sea.*
There are large plains...
People grow...

ACTIVITY 10

The adjectives in the passage, their opposites, other adjectives to describe people/things/objects/animals, etc. in pictures other than the map, comparative and superlative degrees are some of the items that can be used to devise grammar and vocabulary exercises. Verbs in the passage and other verbs (in the present tense) used to take about daily routine can also be practised. Demonstratives such as, that, this, these, those and co-referentials can also be dealt with.

ACTIVITY 11

Examples of activities are given below.

a. Given a picture of the members of a family or of five friends, students could be asked to listen to the description of one of the people in the picture which the teacher could read out to them.
   They could then be asked who the teacher has described.
   The students could also form groups of 8 or 10 and take turns to describe the others in the picture to the members in their group.
   You could use the following framework.
   Describe:
   i. the height of the person—(tall and thin or tall and big-built, or short and shin or short and plump or short and stout)
   ii. their features—face (round/plump/oval/pointed)
   eyes (small/large/round/narrow)
   colour of eyes (black/brown/grey/green)
   nose (pointed/long/sharp/hooked)
   chin (pointed/dimpled)
   lips (thin/thick)
   mouth (small/wide)
   forehead (broad/narrow)
   iii. their hair—black or brown or grey or red
   long or short, straight or wavy or curly thick (long plait)
   iv. the clothes they are wearing (sari and blouse/salwar kameez/long skirt and short blouse/dhoti and kurta/ pants and shirt/T-shirt)
b. Given a coloured picture of six or seven birds, students could be asked to describe the birds. The teacher could describe one bird as an example and the students could be asked to identify the bird. Then each student in a group could describe one of the birds in the picture and the other members of the group asked to identify it (that's the one on the left/it's the bird above the big bird). They could describe the birds along the following lines:
   Sizc: big, small, tiny, large, huge

Beak: small, hooked, sharp, long, pointed, curved
Neck: long, small, thick
Eyes: bead-like, small, slit, large and round, sharp
Feet: webbed (as those of a duck), small, large (with sharp claws)
Colour of: the wings, the head, and 'crest' (a group of feathers that stand up on top of a bird's head) if any, the tail, breast
Alternatively, students could describe animals in a picture.

c. Students could describe the house/flat they live in or their school. (north, south, on the right, left, behind…)

Activity 12

Vocabulary activities could include dictionary work with particular focus on the following words and expressions: amazed, creates, good-will, inclination, concrete, revelries, competitive, deduce, patriotism, prestige, disgraced, savage, combative instincts, aroused, mimic, warfare and attitude.

Grammar activities could include exercises in 'if' clauses and tense forms of regular and irregular verbs.

All the words listed for dictionary work could be used for pronunciation activities.

Group Activity 1

a. Ask students to read the first paragraphs carefully. Then pick out two sentences that express the general point of view.
b. Does the author agree with this point of view?
c. Pick out the word that indicates what the author's point of view regarding the general opinion is.
d. Pick out the sentence which expresses the author's point of view.

Group Activity 2

a. Students read paragraph carefully.
b. Pick out two sentences that further explain why they author holds that opinion about sports
c. What does the author mean by the following statements? First discuss in your own group and then tell the other groups your views.
   i. 'you play to win'
   ii. 'play simply for fun and exercise …'
   iii. Which of the statements above do you think should be a sports person's motto? Why?

d. Discuss why sports become highly competitive.
e. According to the author when is it possible to play simply for fun and exercise.
f. Say, whether the following statements are 'true' or 'false' with reference to the passage you have just read.
    i. The players are responsible for the rivalry between two nations at the international level.
    ii. Nations seriously believe that winning a game is a national virtue.
    iii. It is possible to play imply for the fun and exercise when a feeling of nationalism is aroused.
    iv. All sports nowadays are competitive and players play only to win.
    v. It is possible to play simply for fun and exercise if no feelings of local patriotism are involved.

Activity 13

a. Expressing one's opinion
b. Agreeing/disagreeing with points of view
c. Seeking clarification regarding someone's point of view

Activity 14

Given below are some sample exercises that will help students express their own point of view regarding sport.

Group Activity

The members of each group express their opinion about sports today, and give at least two reasons with examples to support their point of view.

a. They could use expression such as:
   'I think sports ... because ...'
   'In my opinion sports ...for example, ...'
   'I don't think sports should ... because ...'
   'I agree/don't agree with ...that sports ...because/for two reasons...'
b. They could also use expressions such as the following to try and understand what the other members of the group mean (seek clarification):
   'I didn't quite get what you said ...'
   'Could you repeat what you said please.'
   'D'you mean ...'
   'Did you say that ...?'
c. To clarify students could use expressions such as:
   'No that's not what I meant...'

'What I mean is...'
'Let me explain what I meant.'

Activity 16 (Follow-up)

Ask groups of students to agree/disagree with any one of the following statements. Give them guidance in the form of some points for and some against a statement.

a. 'The mobile phone empowers India'.
b. 'A ban on smoking, in public places can successfully rid people of the habit.'
c. 'Money is the root of all evil.'
d. 'Television is doing us a great deal of harm.'
e. 'Warfare only results in loss of life causes destruction and leads to hatred among the nations of the world.'

An example of the points that can emerge from the discussion is given below.

'The mobile phone empowers India.'

Here are some views on the mobile phone expressed by Indians in the Times of India, dated September 14, 2008. You tell your group whether you consider the mobile phone useful and whether it empowers India.

For	Against
1. Yes. India is mobile today! Thanks to the mobile phone. This small gizmo has revolutionised the common man's life. It has not only become a source for 'being always connected' but also become man's best friend.	1. As per Indian psyche, we tend to overdo everything and spoil it eventually. Every Tom, Dick and Harry owns a mobile and flaunts it. Exasperating ringtones are a real nuisance. Service providers fleece the customers while the network is still wanting.
2. Technology surely has its uses and mobile phones are no exception. They are a big boost to communication.	2. Of course, mobile is a means of communication, but it's also become a curse. Frequent calls disturb the peace both at home and in the work place. They can also cause road accidents.
3. Mobile phones are a way of life today. They have become a necessity. They have helped increase people's efficiency at work.	3. Mobile phones have become more of a nuisance today—'Talk more, work less'. They have only, served to fill manufacturers' coffers and unnecessarily make all the sundry feel important. They've made students lazy. Their rapid increase in number has robbed them of any relevance.

Students could begin like this:
'Yes, I think mobiles are ...'
'I agree with the view that mobiles ...'
'I don't think the mobile is ...'
'In my opinion mobile phones...'
'The mobile phone is very useful but ...'
'There is no doubt the mobile phone is necessary, but...'

Activity 17

The following are the functions and the expressions used to perform them.

a. Enquiring: 'How's your.....'
b. Seeking advice: 'What should I do? 'I don't know what to do.'
c. Giving advice: 'I think you ought to ...'
   'I don't think ...'
   'I'd advise you to ...'
   'you should ...'
   'you need to ...'
   'you'd better ...'
d. Accepting advice: 'That's a good idea'
   'I'll certainly give it a try.'
e. Thanking: 'Thank you so much'
f. Responding to thanks: 'Not at all.'
g. Agreeing: 'Indeed it is.'

Activity 18

The following are examples of activities that could be used to reinforce these functions.

a. Ask students to pick out the expressions used for seeking advice and giving advice.
b. Ask students to complete the missing parts of some dialogues given part of the advice in brackets.

Examples of dialogues are given below.

i. A: You're late again.
   B: I'm so sorry. I don't know what I should do to be punctual.
   A: ....(wake up early, pack your bag every evening)

ii. A: What's the matter?
   B: I have a bad headache and a cold.

A: .... (go home and rest)

iii. A: I've been chosen for the interschool badminton tournament.
B: ...... (practice regularly/hard if you want to succeed)

iv. A: Did you read the news?
B: No. Anything serious?
A: Yes. Guwahati is flooded
B: That's awful.
A: .... (postpone your journey)

c. Ask students to enact the dialogues they have completed.

Activity 19

Examples of activities that ensure these functions are performed appropriately are given below.

a. Prepare two dialogues in which one person seeks advice and the other person gives advice. Leave blank spaces for the expressions used to seek advice and give advice and ask students fill them in with appropriate expressions chosen from those given in a box.
b. Ask students to enact the dialogues.
c. Create contexts to enable students to write dialogues in which they use expressions to seek advice and give it.

Given below are some sample contexts:

a.
   i. You are upset because your best friend is annoyed with you for letting him/her down by dropping out of an excursion at the weekend.
   ii. You tell your mother about it and seek her advice.
   iii. Your mother advises you to apologise to him/her and explain that you couldn't come because you were quite ill.
   iv. You thank your mother.

b.
   i. You are very sad.
   ii. Your teacher asks you why you look so sad.
   iii. You tell your teacher that your parents want you to discontinue your studies.
   iv. Your teacher asks why.
   v. You say that they cannot afford to pay the fees for higher studies.
   vi. Your teacher advises you to apply for a merit scholarship. She says you are sure to get it.
   vii. You accept your teacher's advice and thank him/her.

c.
   i. Your friend did not go for tuition on Thursday. You ask him where he was.
   ii. He says he went to watch a cricket match.
   iii. You ask him whether he took his parent's permission.
   iv. He says he didn't.
   v. You tell him that the tutor would let them know you were absent.
   vi. He says his father would be very upset if he came to know about it. He asks you what he should do?
   vii. You tell him it would be best to tell his parents the truth and apologise for not taking their permission, and promise not to do it again.
   viii. He says he certainly will, and thanks you for your advice.

d. Students could enact the dialogues they write.

Activity 20

Given below is a list of expressions used to perform these functions.

a. Enquiring:
   How are you/they?
   How is he/she?
   How have you been?
   How's your + noun + (faring, doing,...).
      sister
      brother
      practice
      business
   How's it going?

b. Giving advice:
   You should...
   You('ll) need to...
   You/they must...
   It would be best to + verb (finite).

c. Accepting advice:
   Yes, you're right.
   I/we (certainly) will...
   Thanks for your advice.
   Yes, I didn't think of that. Thanks.
   Thank you. That didn't occur to me.

d. Thanking:
   Thanks very much.
   I appreciate what you've done for me.
   I can't thank you enough.
   I'm thankful for (all that you've done/your help/patience...).

I will always remember (your kindness/what you've done for me).
I will never forget...

e. Responding to thanks:
   You're welcome. (for a favour done)
   My pleasure.
   Sure.
   Anytime.
f. Agreeing with someone:
   I agree with you.
   You're right.
   You're absolutely right
   I think so too.
   I couldn't agree with you more.

Activities can be prepared along the lines discussed above to teach students the use of expressions to seek advice, give advice and accept advice.

Activity 21

Some sample contexts are given below.

Making suggestions

Ask the students to suggest ways in which the class could celebrate Teacher's Day.

Agreeing and disagreeing

Each member of the group could agree/disagree with the suggestions made by other members of the group on a subject of choice.

Talking about past events

Given a series of pictures (numbered) the students could be asked to tell a story based on the pictures (use of the present continuous).

They could then be asked to narrate the story without the help of the pictures using the past tense.

Expressing likes and dislikes

Students could be asked to express their likes and dislikes regarding colours, food, pets, subjects of study, etc.

for speakers of Hindi
Part 2
SPOKEN ENGLISH
A Foundation Course
KAMLESH SADANAND
SUSHEELA PUNITHA

With Audio
CD

for speakers of Hindi
Part 1
SPOKEN ENGLISH
A Foundation Course
KAMLESH SADANAND
SUSHEELA PUNITHA

Making comparisons

a. Students can be asked to compare two or three stories in their textbooks using comparatives like short/ shorter than, easy/easier/the easiest to remember, interesting /more interesting/the most interesting, better/best, etc.
b. Students can be asked to describe a friend or cousin to their classmates by comparing him/her with classmates. They could use the following expressions: taller than/ not as tall as/short/as tall as/thin/thinner than/not as thin as/(colour) eyes/as large as/not so (large/fair) as, etc.
c. Students could be asked to compare pictures that appear to be similar but in fact are different in many ways. (comparative degree of: long, high, low, big, broad, bright [of colours], etc.,)

Activity 23

Given below are some techniques that could be used to teach students the concept of time.

a. Use a clock (ideally one that chimes) with the seconds hand in addition to the minute and hour hands.
b. Let students listen to the ticking of the clock—to show that time is moving forward.
c. Show that each ticking sound is the smallest unit of sound. After ticking sixty times, the minute hand moves once, and makes up one minute. Every five minutes the minute hand moves to the next.
d. Move the minute hand right round to show that sixty minutes make one hour. Then, show how the hour hand moves to the next number.
e. Explain that every fifteen minutes are equal to one fourth of an hour.

Activity 24

a. Teach students to recognise the hour.
b. Teach them to recognise the half-hour (half past).
c. Teach them to recognise the quarter hour (one fifteen, 'fifteen past, a quarter past).
d. Teach them to recognise a quarter to the hour (fifteen minutes to …, a quarter to …, one forty-five).
e. Teach them to tell the time using the alternative expressions.